A GANGSTA'S EMPIRE 4

**Lock Down Publications &
Ca$h Presents**
*A Gangsta's Empire 4
By Tranay Adams*

.

Lock Down Publications

P.O. Box 870494
Mesquite, Tx 75187

Visit our website at **www.lockdownpublications.com**

First Edition December 2019
Printed in the United States of America
This is a work of fiction. Names, characters, places, and incidents either are products of the author's imagination or are used fictitiously. Any similarity to actual events or locales or persons, living or dead, is entirely coincidental.

Cover design and layout by: Dynasty's Cover Me
Book interior design by: Shawn Walker
Edited by: Shon Progue

Tranay Adams

Stay Connected with Us!

Text **LOCKDOWN** to 22828 to stay up-to-date with new releases, sneak peaks, contests and more…

Thank you!

Submission Guideline.

Submit the first three chapters of your completed manuscript to ldpsubmissions@gmail.com, subject line: Your book's title. The manuscript must be in a .doc file and sent as an attachment. Document should be in Times New Roman, double spaced and in size 12 font. Also, provide your synopsis and full contact information. If sending multiple submissions, they must each be in a separate email.

Have a story but no way to send it electronically? You can still submit to LDP/Ca$h Presents. Send in the first three chapters, written or typed, of your completed manuscript to:

LDP: Submissions Dept
Po Box 870494
Mesquite, Tx 75187

DO NOT send original manuscript. Must be a duplicate.

Provide your synopsis and a cover letter containing your full contact information.

Thanks for considering LDP and Ca$h Presents.

Tranay Adams

CHAPTER ONE

Valdez and his best friend, Sleepy, stood beside his Lincoln Navigator on big ass 26-inch chrome rims. They passed a smoldering blunt between themselves as they waited for Gerardo to arrive.

"'Sup witchu, foo? You seem worried." Sleepy asked as he took the half smoked Backwoods away from Valdez. He was a five-foot-five dude with a big head and eyes that made him look like he was always sleepy, but he was actually high most of the time. He wore a Raiders beanie pulled low over his eyes and an oversized black sweatshirt.

Sleepy said this because he saw Valdez with the worried look on his face, tapping his foot impatiently and checking his surroundings every two minutes.

"Yeah, I'm fucking worried, Vato, you know how my bro is. He seemed to be really pissed off about Maul being killed. You know that foos were locked up together, and Maul became like a son to 'em." Valdez told him.

"I hear you, bro, but chill out. That's yo brother, it's not like he's gonna kill you of something." He passed him back the Backwood and he took it. At that moment, two shining orbs were approaching them from the opening of the warehouse, placing them in the spotlights. The bright lights caused their faces to ball up and they held their hand above their eyebrows, trying to see who it was advancing in their direction. They concluded that it was Gerardo inside of the white Mercedes-Benz limousine. The stretched vehicle stopped, and sure enough, Gerardo stepped out of the car, making his way towards Valdez and Sleepy. He stopped eight feet away from them, staring directly at Valdez; he folded his arms across his chest.

"Alright, mijo, talk," Gerardo told him, standing there, wearing a hard face. As he listened to a stuttering Valdez, he began to pace the floor while holding his hands behind his back, head bowed. Valdez kept his watchful eyes on him as he filled him in about everything that had happened during the war. The nigga Valdez was fearful because he knew how brazen the shot caller could be when he was given bad news.

"Tell me something, Valdez," Gerardo said as he reached inside of his snazzy suit and pulled out a chrome, pearl handle .45 automatic handgun with a silencer on its barrel.

"Yes, bro?" Valdez wiped the sweat from off his forehead. You see, Valdez wasn't actually the leader of the BDOG; he was an underboss. He was the man to holler at if you needed to get anything to Gerardo. The nigga commanded the soldiers and made sure the work got in their hands. Homeboy captained the streets while Gerardo made sure he got all of the drugs he needed.

"Who gave Maul the okay to get at Jabar, huh? Who gave my cousin the go ahead to carry out that hit?" Gerardo took a sip of his liquor, keeping a watchful eye on Valdez the entire time.

Valdez's eyes grew big and he swallowed the lump of nervousness in his throat as he fidgeted with his fingers. He continued to sweat bullets as he tried to gather his wits and respond to the question the head honcho asked. "Well, uh, well, I did, bro. I told him it was okay to go ahead with whacking out Jabar."

"You gave 'em the nod without getting up with me first?" Gerardo asked as he mad dogged Valdez. He was visibly upset now. He'd stopped pacing the floor and ran his hand down his face. His tanned face was tinted rose pedal red, his eyebrows were arched and his nose was scrunched up.

"Bro, I thought chu made me your second in command so I could take care of the street business." Valdez reasoned.

"Yeah, I did but I thought you'd have more sense than to give Maul the assignment, knowing that I was trying to keep him outta trouble not get 'em in it."

"But he insisted because his cousin, Victor, got killed!"

At this time, Sleepy was still smoking the blunt, looking back and forth between the brothers. Out of the blue, Gerardo's arm shot up, pointing his chrome .45 at Valdez' face. The youngsta's eyes bulge and his mouth dropped open. He nearly pissed himself seeing his brother pulling the trigger of his gun.

Poc!

The back of Sleepy's skull splattered against the side of the Navigator's front passenger's window, sliding down into the windowsill. A dead Sleepy dropped down to his knees, eyes voided of life and mouth open. He fell flat on his face, Backwood lying beside him on the ground burning, smoke rising into the air.

"Oh, my, my God!" Valdez' eyes were as big as tennis balls. His hands were shaking at his face. There were specks of blood on the side of his face from Sleepy standing near him when he was popped. Tears pooled Valdez's eyes and ran down his face. He kneeled down to Sleepy and lifted his head by the neck causing chunks of his bloody brain to fall out of the hole in the back of his skull. He stood there on his knees holding his best friend in his arms crying, teardrops splashing on his dead face. He kissed him on the cheek and swept his eyelids closed with the palm of his hand. Afterwards, he laid him back down, removed his jacket and draped it over him, leaving only his legs sticking out.

Gerardo approached Valdez and gave him an unwanted one armed hug, kissing him on the top of his head. He told him he loved him dearly and then rubbed the back of his head, looking him in his eyes. "You love your big brother too, right, mijo?" Valdez looked at him fumingly, wanting to beat his ass, but he knew he'd probably kill him for laying a paw on him so he checked his hanger. He shut his eyelids briefly and took a deep breath, calming himself the best way he could. Looking up at his brother, he nodded and told him he loved him. "Good. I'm sorry I had to kill yo best amigo, but I had to teach you a lesson." Gerardo replied, he then used the end of his suit's jacket to wipe his fingerprints off of the murder weapon and handed it to him. "Get rid of this piece and his body. I'll get back witchu tomorrow." He hugged him again and kissed him. Once he patted him on his back, he took off walking back towards the Mercedes-Benz limousine. He climbed in and slammed the door behind him. A moment later the fancy stretch vehicle was driving out of the old warehouse.

Once Gerardo was back behind the limousine tinted window glass, he pulled out his trusty Zippo lighter and a Cuban cigar roasting it until it wafted with smoke. He sucked on the end of it and blew out a big ass cloud of smoke, looking to his lovely wife, Marla. Marla's eyes were focused out of the passenger window. Gerardo could see the reflection of her face through the glass and he knew that something was troubling her, only he didn't know what.

"What's the matter, sweetheart?" Gerardo asked as he gripped her manicured hand and caressed her knuckles affectionately. He hated to see her looking how she was. If it was something bothering her then he always made it his business to fix it.

Marla looked to him with tears in his eyes. "I'm worried about her."

"I promise you, beloved, everything will be fine. No harm will come to her."

"You shouldn't make promises that you can't keep." She said as tears slid down her cheeks. Switching hands with the Cuban cigar he was holding, Gerardo used his other hand to whip out his handkerchief and dab his lady's cheeks dry.

"Tell me what you want me to do to make this better. You tell me exactly what you expect of me."

"I want you to promise you won't come at this Jabar character again until she's safe and sound. Can you do that?"

Gerardo took a puff of his cigar as he thought about it and said, "I promise you that we'll make sure no harm comes to her, when the shit finally hits the fan. I give you my word. I put my life on it. How's that?"

"Okay. That's good enough." She told him. "But I wanna go see her...soon. I mean, real soon."

"Notta problem at all, that's something that can be arranged." He pulled her close and kissed her. He then caressed her cheek with the side of his hand and kissed her on the forehead. She snuggled up under him and shut her eyelids, drifting off to sleep. He continued to puff on his illegal cigar; blowing smoke rings out into the air.

The next morning

Dough Boy pulled his truck up inside of the parking lot of the car wash. He handed the short Mexican man who was wearing a navy blue NY baseball cap and a faded blue T-shirt a twenty dollar bill. The Mexican man took the dub and scribbled down something on a small notepad. Once he'd finished scribbling down what Dough Boy wanted done to his SUV, he tore off the lower half of the slip of paper and handed it to his customer. This was his receipt.

"Good looking out, my nigga," Dough Boy glanced at the receipt. He then tapped Voss and told him 'come on'. The best friends hopped out of the enormous vehicle and made their way over to the tint which a row of chairs sat under, providing shade. Not too far away from the tint there was a food truck that a grip of Mexican people was at buying Spanish food.

"Yo, I'ma get me a coke from off this truck, you want something?" Voss asked him.

"Yeah," Dough Boy said as he massaged his chin, staring at the menu which was plastered on the side of the food truck. "Get me four tacos, and a horchata."

"Fa sho," Voss walked out to retrieve him and his home-boy's order.

While Voss was busy at the food truck, Dough Boy turned his attention to the Mexican cats that were lathering the cars with soap which were all on line. As they were tending to the cars more automobiles were pulling up. There was a Nissan Sentra, a Dodge Charger, an Explorer Sport and then, finally, a 2018 royal blue Chevrolet Impala. A scrawny nigga rocking a blue bandana around his head and a wife beater hopped out. He paid for his car to be washed and made his way over in Dough Boy's direction. The platinum necklace hanging from around his neck held to a diamond flooded hand which was throwing up a *C* which stood for Crip.

The necklace swung from left to right as homeboy advanced toward the shaded area. Off top Dough Boy knew that homeboy rocking the bandana was J.D. The nigga that was basically running the shit on the other side of the color spectrum. He could tell by his scowling face that he was hot about something. If he had to guess he'd say that it was about his shot caller God Body getting popped. With the shot caller out of the way, that left his people without a supply on dope so they could eat.

Hearing the front passenger door of the Chevrolet Impala slam shut, Dough Boy looked beyond J.D. and saw a big ass nigga in all black. He was rocking a fedora, black sunglasses, and a black Dickie suit. The nigga looked like Ving Rhames in the face, and by the way he was adjusting his pants on his waistline he knew that he was packing. There wasn't any doubt in Dough Boy's mind that the Ving Rhames looking mothafucka was J.D.'s bodyguard, Hog.

Voss had just stepped to Dough Boy with his plate of tacos and his drink when J.D. and that nigga Hog stopped before them.

"What's up, my nigga? How's the wife and kid?" Voss asked J.D. as he cracked open the red Coca Cola can and took a sip. While this was going on, Dough Boy was taking a bite of his taco and keeping a close eye on Hog. If homeboy decided to get stupid then he was coming off the hip spitting hot shit.

"Cuz, fuck all the pleasantries," J.D. waved him off. "Nigga, them bitchez you sent at my OG wasn't no fucking strippers, they were hittaz. They split my nigga shit and burned his mansion down!"

Voss shrugged his shoulders and then said, "And?"

"Fuck you mean 'and?' that wasn't the deal, Loc!" J.D. scowled harder and bit down on his bottom lip. His fists were clenched at his sides and bulging with veins.

"This shit is chess. I made my next move my best move. But don't wet it, *Blood*." Voss emphasized on the Blood seeing as how J.D. kept cuzzing and locing him and he was a B-dawg. "You know that dope of ours y'all been dying to get y'all hands on?"

Some of the animosity disappeared from off of J.D.'s face and he folded his arms across his chest. He and his gang had wanted to get their hands on Voss' *Power*. It was the talk of Vegas and all of the dope fiends were hollering at his people to get it. Yeah, J.D. and his people were making money off the dope they had but it was shit compared to what the Bloods on Voss' side was serving. On top of that, they didn't have their shot caller, God Body, to supply them any more so they didn't have any product to get money off of. As of now they were reduced to selling whatever little bullshit they could get from off of small time heroine peddlers and that didn't sit right with J.D. and his goons. They were used to the kind of money that God Body's dope brought in.

"What about it?" J.D. asked curiously.

"Well, I've came up with a price per kilo that I feel we'll both be happy with if you were to buy from me and only me." Voss switched hands with the Coca Cola can and reached into his back pocket and pulled out a business card, handing it to J.D. He watched as J.D. eyed the business card, looking pleased with the price he'd written down. The Crip then flicked the card with his finger and thumb and nodded his head in approval.

"Now, this, I can fuck with this."

"I thought this offer would meet your approval." Voss told him. "Now you buy twenty of them thangz from me up front every month. And everything's a go. Hit me on my hip tomorrow and I'll let chu know where to meet my people with that paypa."

"Okay. Fa sho." J.D. lifted his fist, and they dapped up.

Hearing a horn being blown, Voss looked over to see one of the Mexicans that was lathering up Dough Boy's truck waving his dingy wash rag at them, trying to get their attention.

"That's us, Dough." Voss nudged Dough Boy and they headed toward the truck. "Get at me, big dawg." Voss told J.D.

"At this price. You ain't gotta worry about it, homie. I'ma holla at chu, for real, for real." He flashed him the card before sliding it into his back pocket. He then went ahead and pulled out a cigarette. Hog assisted him in lighting it. J.D. sucked on the butt of the square and blew out a cloud of smoke, watching Voss and Dough Boy drive off. "We're about to make some reallll money fucking with these red rag niggaz, Hog. I'm talking more money than we've ever seen fucking with that nigga God Body. Onna set."

***

Yada lay in bed staring at a portrait of her and Voss hugged up. The feeling of guilt crept upon her and she felt horrible. Although she'd been given the go ahead by Voss to keep Jabar's suspicions from off her, she still couldn't help feeling like she'd betrayed him. All of her life she'd been a one man woman. She'd never cheated or flirted with the opposite sex while she was in a relationship. Now, that she had given Jabar the pussy while she was Voss' wife, she felt grimy, dirty, and filthy.

Suddenly, Yada turned the portrait face down and took Jabar's arm from around her. She hopped out of bed and dashed to the bathroom, slamming the door shut behind her. She opened the glass enclosed shower and twisted the dials, adjusting the temperature of the water to her liking. Afterwards, she stripped down to her nakedness and stepped inside of the shower, shutting the glass door behind her. The hot water created a mist and fogged the glass of the shower.

Yada lathered up a loofa and got to soaping, scrubbing every inch of her body, roughly. The way she was acting you would have sworn that she had bugs or something crawling over her body, but that wasn't the case. It wasn't the actually the dirt that she was scrubbing away, but the betrayal she felt that she'd dealt to Voss. Right there in the shower she vowed not to ever tell Voss about what happened. Although he said he could live with her sleeping with Jabar if she had to, she knew how men were. The thought of another man entering what they deemed was their woman could really fuck with their psyche, whether they'd like to admit it or not.

Yada scrubbed and scrubbed her body, but no matter how roughly she did, she still felt dirty. After a while she broke down sobbing and dropped the loofa. She bowed her head and placed her hands against the tan granite wall. Her body trembled as tears slid down her face and mixed with the spraying water from the showerhead. The hot water rinsed the suds off of Yada and sent it swirling down the drain.

***

A singing Yada moved around the kitchen in her silk pajamas and robe cooking breakfast. The way she was carrying on you wouldn't have think she spent the past forty minutes inside of the shower crying her eyes out. Before she left out of the bathroom she gave herself one hell of a pep talk. She reminded herself what she was doing and what she was doing it for. You see, it wasn't just holding it down for Voss' ass, she was holding it down for LeLe as well. She knew without a shadow of a doubt that if she wouldn't have given Jabar the ass and acted like she was so much in love with him that he would have surely murdered LeLe. And that was something she couldn't allow to happen. LeLe was her bitch. Her ride of die. She loved little mamma more that she loved herself. Besides Voss, she was the only person she had left in the world. If she was to lose her, she'd probably take her own life.

Jabar's ugly ass walked into the kitchen smiling and looking at Yada cooking. He was in a black wife beater and camouflage cargo pants.

"This food smells good then a mothafucka, I didn't know you could burn." Jabar said as he came up from behind LeLe. He wrapped her arms around her waist and started kissing up her neck while flipping over the pancakes in the skillet with the spatula.

Yada cringed and rolled her eyes as soon as she felt Jabar's hands on her. She fought back the urge to throw up and put a smile on her face. "Shit, I hadda come down here and hook my baby up with a lil' something, something after the way he laid it down last night."

"Oh, is that right? Big Daddy laid it down?" he smiled harder having had his ego stroked.

"Like a boss!" she claimed. Jabar wasn't a slouch in the bedroom but he didn't have shit on Voss. She then looked to him and said, "Gemme some lip."

"Mmmmm," Jabar hummed as he kissed Yada deeply. She held the back of his head with one hand as they made out while the other hand held the spatula. Jabar kissed her on the lips once more and smacked her on the ass. He then turned to the island and picked up a crisp strip of bacon lying on a black plate covered with folded up paper towels.

Jabar made his way around the kitchen table pulling his gun from off of his waistline. He sat down at the kitchen table and sat his banga down on the table top. He took out the small walkie talkie and sat it down beside his gun.

"Now, this is real bacon, not that turkey bullshit these God Body mothafuckaz be eating." Jabar exclaimed and took another bite of his bacon.

"That's all I fucks with, baby, the real deal." Yada said as she fixed him a plate.

"Boss dawg, we've gotta woman who's out here wanting to see Yada!" Tankhead's voice came over the walkie talkie.

A frowned up Jabar looked up at Yada who had just set his plate down in front of him. Yada's forehead creased wondering who it was that was there to see her.

"You expecting somebody?" Jabar asked her.

Yada shook her head saying, "No. I don't know who that could be."

"Yo, she's not expecting any company, so see who that broad is."

Yada started feeding Jabar his breakfast as he anxiously a waited to hear back from Tankhead.

"Yoooo, she says her name is Marla. Marla Blanca. She says she's Yada's mother."

"Momma?" Yada's eyes doubled in size and her mouth dropped open. She dropped the fork of eggs into the plate and took off running out of the kitchen, heading to the living room. She pulled open the front door and headed down the steps in a hurry. Huffing and puffing she made her way across the enormous lawn. She tripped and fell on her face hard, wincing. The wind had been knocked out of her but she scrambled to her feet and kept on running. Beads of sweat formed on her forehead and neck. She slipped out of one of her house slippers, hauling ass.

A few more feet later, and the other slipper came off. The mansion, which had armed goons on its rooftop, was growing smaller and smaller behind her now. As she neared the gates she could see a white Mercedes-Benz limousine. She didn't know if it was her mother inside of the luxury vehicle or not but she prayed that it was. She hadn't seen her in years.

By the time Yada had reached the gates, she was sweating profusely. Her shoulders rose and fell as she took in healthy gulps of air. She was exhausted, but it wasn't for nothing. She had to see if the mysterious woman idling outside of her mansion was really the woman that had given birth to her.

"Tankhead, open the gate." Yada ordered. Tankhead ducked inside of the security guard booth and mashed a button that activated the gates. As soon as there was enough room for Yada to slip out between the gates she went through them and approached the backdoor of the lengthy vehicle. She knocked on the tinted black glass. A minute later, the window descended, revealing the passenger inch by inch until the person's face was completely visible.

Yada found herself staring at the beautiful, rich chocolate face of an older woman that resembled her down to a T. The woman had snow white hair that was braided back in eight neat cornrows. She wore a cream-colored overcoat over a matching turtle neck. In her left ear, she sported a hearing-aid which looked like a Blu-Tooth.

"Oh, my God, it's my baby, my baby girl!" Hot tears instantly stung the older woman's eyes as she opened the backdoor and stepped out, one high heel shoe after the other. Yada dropped down to her knees and hugged her mother at the waist, burying her face into her torso. She cried her eyes out. Her head bobbed and her shoulders trembled greatly. All the woman, Marla, could do was hold Yada and cry, occasionally wiping her dripping eyes with the back of her manicured hand.

"I can't believe you're alive. Daddy said that word in the street was that you were dead." Yada told her.

"That's not true. I think your father told you that 'cause he wanted to keep me away from you on the account of that horrible thing I done. I cannot say I blame him either. 'Cause had the shoe been on the other foot, I would have done the same."

"I understand." Yada claimed.

"I'm glad you do, sweetheart." Marla caressed her daughter's back.

As Marla caressed Yada's back, she thought back to the horrible thing she'd done to get her banned from her life. So much had happened since then. But it was that one horrible thing that she regretted the most. She'd never forgive herself for it, but she hoped that one day that Yada would find it in her heart to. That is, if she hadn't already.

A twelve-year-old Yada jerked from left to right trying to break loose from her restraints. Her wrists and ankles were tied to her canopy bed's posts by different colored pillowcases, holding her in place. Having grown exhausted from her futile attempt to escape captivity, Yada went limp and dropped her head back onto the pillow. Her chest jumped up and down as she breathed heavily. Tears filled her eyes and ran out of the corners of them, causing her mascara to run. Her mother had applied makeup to her youthful face, making her look slightly older than she actually was. She was also in a skimpy bathing suit that showed off her still developing body.

Yada tried to scream but the blue bandana in her mouth stopped the sound from escaping. Marla, Yada's mother, kneeled down beside her, hushing her and brushing her hair from out of her face. She was a skinny with ashy skin and sunken eyes that had dark rings around them. She was wearing a navy blue beanie, a valor sweatshirt and a copper brown overcoat. Her lips were ashy and she had white shit at the corners of her mouth. She was in dire need of a hit of crack to get her mind right. At the moment, her husband, who was also a crackhead, Lyndell, was out in the streets looking for a dope boy to rob. He was looking to score enough cash to get feminine products for them, food and crack.

"Shhhh, it's gonna be all right, baby girl. Don't worry. I just need you to do this for me this one time and that's it. Momma really needs yo help. I'm sick. I'm really, really sick." Marla told her.

"Mmmmmmm," Yada screamed no over and over again, whipping her head from side to side, and then trying to pull her wrists and ankles from out of the pillowcases that kept her bound to the posts of the canopy bed. The tears that poured out of her eyes seemed to be coming down in buckets, soaking her cheeks.

"I'm sorry, baby. But I gotta do this. It'll hurt for a minute but then it'll be over before you know it." She kissed her on the forehead and then walked out of the bedroom, closing the door behind her. A moment later, she returned with an Asian gentleman counting up the dead presidents he'd given her. The Asian cat was wearing a hat and a suit, which was beneath an over coat.

"Is this her?" The Asian man asked Marla.

"Yep. That's her. Twelve-years-old, just like I'd promise." Marla folded up the money he'd given her and shoved it into her back pocket. She then pulled a red wrapper to a Trojan condom from out of her pocket. Its edges were worn and showing the silver foil, but the latex was still good. The

Asian man plucked the condom out of Marla's hand and removed his coat, hanging it on the back of the door. Marla left out of the bedroom, leaving the sick mothafucka alone with her daughter. The Asian man set his hat down on the dresser and disrobed, leaving himself in the nude. He had a hairy bush and a limp, shrimp dick. When Yada seen him coming towards her, she screamed and screamed, trying desperately to pull free from her bondages.

"My, whatta sexy young lady you are," Mr. Cho, the Asian man, said as he sat down on the bed beside Yada. He tossed the condom aside because he didn't plan on using it on her. Nah, his perverted mind was determined to go inside of the innocent young girl raw!

Mr. Cho ran his hand up and down Yada's leg and over her thigh. Yada was terrified. She squeezed her eyelids closed and prayed and prayed, feeling her assailant's hand traveling along her body. While Mr. Cho was using his left-hand to grope her underdeveloped form, he used the other to stroke his dick up and down. Before he knew it, his manhood had stiffened. It had veins covering it and pre-cum oozed out of its pale, yellow head. When Yada seen this, her eyelids stretched as wide as they could making her pupils appear smaller than they actually were. Beads of sweat ran down her forehead and she screamed as loud as she could over and over again, but the bandana across her mouth muffled her.

***

Marla leaned up against the side of the door of the bedroom where Mr. Cho and Yada was, taping her foot impatiently and glancing at the clock on the wall. She couldn't wait until the Asian man got his rocks off so she could rush *him out and see about catching up with one of the crack dealers on the block before they took it in for the night. It had been a while since she had gotten high, so the minutes that did go by felt like hours. The wait was driving her insane and she didn't know how long she could take it.*

Hearing the doorknob of the front door rattling as it was being unlocked, Marla looked to it. She hoped and prayed that it wasn't her husband, Lyndell, coming through the door. But she knew it had to be him because no one else had the keys to the house. Lyndell emerged through the door with a brown paper bag. He was whistling Dixie. When he saw Marla, he smiled at her and showed all of his missing teeth, dangling a bundle of tan crack rocks before her eyes.

"We 'bouta get as high as the moon tonight, baby." Lyndell danced inside of the kitchen and sat the bag down on the table. He got his mangled crack pipe out that had the burned endings on it and a worn Bic lighter. He stuffed his pipe with the crack rock and was about to fire it up, but then he looked around the house. His eyebrows rose when he didn't see Yada anywhere in sight. "Where's baby girl at?"

Marla's eyes grew big as she looked around nervously, heart thudding crazily in her chest, she stammered, "She's, uh, uh, uh..."

While Marla was stammering, Lyndell's eyes shot over to the coffee table. He found Mr. Cho's briefcase sitting beside it. His eyes then shot to the master bedroom door. He knew something was up, so he drew his old Colt .45 from his waistline and made his way towards the bedroom door. Marla grabbed hold of his arm and he shoved her away, causing her to flip over the couch and fall onto the floor. He kicked at the door's lock as hard as he could. On the third kick, the door of the master bedroom flew open and he rushed inside.

When he turned to the bed he spotted Mr. Cho straddled over his daughter, about to slip himself inside of her. When the Asian man saw him his heart quickened and he threw his hands up into the air. His eyes were wide and his mouth was hanging wide open. He was scared as shit. Before that sleazy mothafucka could say anything, Lyndell gripped his pistol with both hands and pointed it.

Pow, pow!

Mr. Cho grimaced and grabbed his stomach, falling awkwardly out of the bed and onto the floor. He bawled in pain and whined like a fucking sissy. A shadow eclipsed him and he looked up, to see Lyndell standing over him with his .45 pointed down at him. Lyndell mad dogged him and popped one in his noodle, splattering his blood and brain fragments on the surface.

After he laid out Mr. Cho, Lyndell untied his daughter from the bed posts. He then slipped his shirt from over his head and put it on her. She hugged him and buried her face into his wife beater, sobbing loud and hard. Yada's body trembled as Lyndell held her in one of his arms, his other hand holding tight to his murder weapon.

"Shhhhh, there, there, baby girl, I got chu. I got chu. Everything is going to be all right." Lyndell kissed her on top of her head.

Scowling, he looked to the door and saw Marla. She was looking guilty and afraid. Right then, Lyndell eased away from Yada and speed walked over to Marla. He grabbed her by her throat, lifting her up to the tips of her raggedy sneakers and slamming her up against the wall. He then placed the barrel of his pistol inside of her grill, causing her to gag on it. Her palms became sweaty and her heart raged, beating out of control.

24

"Bitch, you sell our daughter's innocence so you can get high? I'ma blow a fucking hole through the back of yo' head," Lyndell swore as he cocked the hammer back on his old, beat-up revolver. Still holding his .45 in Marla's mouth, Lyndell took a step back, looking her dead in her terrified eyes. He slowly began to pull back the trigger of his revolver.

"Daddy, noooo!" Yada grabbed him by his other arm. She looked up at him teary-eyed. He looked down at her and she said, "Please, daddy, don't kill her. Please."

Lyndell looked back up at Marla scowling harder at her and clenching his jaws. It seemed like he was staring into her eyes for an eternity, before he took his .45 out of her mouth and fired a shot near her left ear. Marla howled in agony as she doubled over, holding her left ear. She winced harder and harder, hearing the eerie ringing sound in her ear. The sound threw off her equilibrium and she fell to the floor, seeing her husband and daughter standing over her.

"Grab your things, we've gotta get outta here, baby girl. Hurry up." Lyndell told Yada.

"Where are we going to go? Are we taking mommy with us?" Yada asked, looking between her parents.

"I'm not sure of where we're going yet. I'll think of a place along the way. As far as your mother is concerned, from this day forward, you'll never see her again."

"But, daddy..." Yada was cut off by her agitated father.

Lyndell's head snapped in Yada's direction and he said, "No, buts, baby girl, grab your things so we can get outta here, now!"

Yada ran back and forth across the bedroom grabbing what little belongings she had. She ran over to her mother. Kneeling down to her, she kissed her on the cheek and told her she loved her. Yada then stood upright and wiped her dripping eyes with the back of her hand. Her father grabbed her by her hand and they fled out of the house, hearing sirens as police cars raced up the block.

Marla escaped from the house that night and took refuge in a warehouse that had been shut down for some time. She smoked up the crack that Lyndell had given her, and a few days later found herself a pimp who put her on the blade.

***

Krueger pulled up on Figueroa which was known for its prostitute activity. He played the shade beneath a tree and blended in with the night. For a time, he just sat back watching the hookers coming and going as Johns pulled up negotiating prices for sex. With a keen eye he probed the blade looking for something to his liking. He spotted Marla wearing a Cleopatra wig. She wore a net dress that made her white bra and panties visible. Over all of this, she sported a charcoal gray trench coat that hung just passed her white leather hooker boots. She tapped her heel against the sidewalk and chewed bubble gum, occasionally blowing bubbles with it. Krueger wanted her in the worse way. It wasn't because he found her attractive. Nah, it was because she resembled his late wife almost down to the T.

You see, eight months ago, Krueger had snapped when he found out his wife threatened to file for divorce and take their two kids. The thought of losing them was just too much for him to bear and he killed them all, shooting them all at point blank range, execution style. After the deed was done, he set them all up inside of the basement, convincing himself mentally that they were still alive. But that couldn't have been further from the truth. That mothafucka had just lost his mind. These days, Krueger found himself yearning to be with his family, especially his wife. He was missing her so much that he found himself out in the city on a nightly basis, stalking ho strolls and picking up prostitutes that resembled his darling, Chazetta.

Krueger flashed his headlights of his car twice, to get Marla's attention. When the light shined on and off of her face she looked in his direction then to her pimp. He was a fairly tall black dude with 360 waves and pretty boy looks. He rocked a leather jacket and starched jeans. The nigga was pretending to be on a phone call as he watched the block for police presence. Seeing that the coast was clear, he gave Marla the nod and she started in the direction of Krueger's car. She combed her fingers through her hair and popped her gum. Reaching the front passenger side window, she knocked on the glass and smiled. Krueger smiled back at her and descended the window.

"Hey, handsome, ya lookin' for a good time?" Marla crossed her wrists at the windowsill and her manicured hands hung inside of the vehicle.

"Fuckin' aye."

Marla smiled and chewed. "Alright, handsome, what kinda party are ya looking for?"

Krueger didn't say a mothafucking thing; he just held up a vial of crack and wagged it before her eyes. Marla licked her lips and tried to snatch it from him, but he pulled it back, teasing her. She looked from the crack vial to her pimp who had his eyes on her.

"Alright, what is it that you want?" she asked Krueger.

"H and A, doll."

"It's sixty for head and two-hundred for ass."

"Let's party then."

Marla hopped into the front passenger seat and slammed the door shut behind her. She took her crack pipe from out of her purse and stuffed it with some of the off white crack rocks from out of Krueger's vial. Once she was done, she set the crack vial down inside of the ashtray and pulled out her trusty Bic lighter. She produced a bluish flame with a yellow tip, holding it to the tip of the crack pipe and sucking on the end of it. Marla's cheeks swelled and she took drags from the crack pipe and then blew out a big ass cloud of smoke. While she was doing this, she directed Krueger to an alley where they could get busy.

Marla then went back to smoking on the crack pipe. Before she knew it, that nigga Krueger was pulling into the dark alley. Enjoying the effects of the potent drug, Marla took her lips away from the crack pipe and smiled with her eyelids shut. When she peeled them back open, they were moist and glassy.

Krueger unzipped his jeans and pulled out his meat. Taking the crack pipe from Marla, he sat it in the ashtray and invited her over to his dick.

"Hold on, handsome." Marla pulled out a gold foiled square that had Magnum scrolled across it in black letters. Tearing it open with her teeth, she pulled the lubricated condom out from its jail and tossed its wrapper aside. Pulling her hair back into a ponytail, Marla grabbed his dick and brought her pink lip sticked lips to it. She slid the rubber down over his endowment and worked it on him with expertise. Having done this, she used both of her hands to smooth the off white latex down over him and make sure that there wasn't any air bubbles in it. Soon after, Marla was whipping her head on him and sending her hot river of saliva pouring down his shaft.

She didn't have a gag reflex as she took all of him inside of her mouth until his mound met with her chin. It was there that she hummed a tone that vibrated his meat and drove him crazy. Spitting his penis back out, Marla spat on it and jerked it off to get it stiffer than it was before. She spat on his thang again, leaving a length of saliva that was attached to her bottom lip. Afterwards, Marla threw lips to his shit and he pressed his hand to the back of her head. Her dome bobbed up and down his cock making sloshing noises. He threw his head back and his eyelids flickered. Her mouth felt good. So good that he thought that he saw the thick wooden doors of Heaven open and light shining on his face.

"I'm sorry, Chazetta," Krueger's eyes pooled with tears and he sniffled. "I'm so sorry, baby. I wish I could take it back...I wish that I could take it all back." He broke down slobbering and sobbing and Marla kept on sucking on him. Suddenly, Krueger found his swipe tingling and his head bobbed a little bit. His eyes became hooded and he licked his lips, as snot peeked out of his nose. He snorted that shit back up though. "Awwww, shit! Awww, fuck, baby, you doing me so good!" he looked down at the blonde as her head jumped up and down. "I don't know how...oh, God," he threw his head back and his eyes rolled to their whites.

His mouth moved animatedly and his lips quivered, as he felt himself about to explode. Abruptly, he threw his head back up to watch Marla work that platinum tongue of hers. His cheek slicked wet from tears of guilt and he licked his lips. "...I don't know how...how I ever let something as beautiful as my family get pulled into my nightmare. If I could...Ooooooo," his face twitched and he felt his dick head throbbing at the back of her throat. "Sssssssss, Jesus, fuuuuuuck..." he began stroking the hair on the back of her head.

"If I could give my life to bring you all back I would. Oh, I swear to Goddddd that I would." Krueger squeezed the back of her neck and pushed himself up from the floor.

Lifting his ass up from the driver seat, he fucked her mouth fast and furiously. His powerful thrusts caused her to gag like she was pushing a toothbrush too far to the back of her mouth. A minute later it happened; he bucked like crazy and held her down on his pipe. Marla struggled to pull herself up slapping and crawling at his face but he wasn't letting that ass up until he released his children inside of the condom.

Krueger squeezed his eyelids shut and clenched his jaws tightly. His face rippled with wrinkles and he threw his head back. He busted off long and hard, bucking like a Bronco in his seat. He took his hand from off of Marla's head and she tossed her head back. Her eyeliner ran from her crying and she spit out his semen. She wiped her mouth with her fist and looked to the nigga'z dick. The head of his dick was sticking out of the top of the condom. It was ruined.

"You fucking asshole!" Marla screamed and threw wild punches at him. He threw up his arms and blocked most of the assault. Breathing heavily and still pissed off, Marla grabbed her purse and hopped out of the car. Krueger looked over his shoulder through the tinted window and could see her hurrying across the street looking both ways. She waved to her pimp who was still at the telephone booth and told him what had happened. Marla pointed in his direction and he scowled. Together, they went speed walking in the direction of Krueger's vehicle. Swiftly, Krueger pulled the busted rubber off of him and zipped up his jeans. Once he grabbed that Act Right from beneath the seat, he threw open the driver side door and hopped out. He saw Marla and her pimp coming up on him as he rounded his whip. The first thing he noticed was the man's threatening eyes and the .9mm in his hand.

"You disrespectin' my bitch, mu'fucka?" the pimp spat.

"Pop his ass, daddy!" Marla yelled.

"You dead, nigga!" the pimp hollered, spittle jumping from off his lips.

At the exact same time, the flesh peddler and Krueger lifted their burners but the White nigga was just a little faster on the draw. There were golden orange flashes in their faces as they both got off. The pimp got off one shot while the Krueger got off several more, lighting his mothafucka chest up. The man danced on his feet a second before dropping his gun and greeting the curb. His eyes took a far off look and his head fell off to the side. His last breath escaped his mouth and his blood soaked chest went completely still.

"Ah! Ahhh! Ahhhh!" Marla screamed bloody murder with her trembling hands cupping her face. Veins were at her temples as she continued shrill loud enough to wake up the entire neighborhood. It wasn't until Krueger pointed that thang at her face that she shut her dick suckers. She swallowed the ball of nervousness in her throat and stood where she was frozen solid. "Oh, please, please don't kill me." she dropped down to her knees with her hands together begging.

Krueger lowered his weapon at her thinking cap and settled his finger on the trigger. Gritting, he squeezed his eyelids shut and peeled them back open repeatedly. His mind was playing tricks on him. For some goddamn reason he kept seeing his wife's face on hers. The face would go from his loving wife to the Marla's. This confused the fuck out of him and caused him to tap his foot involuntarily. There was a war going on inside of his brain and he didn't know what side of him was going to win.

"Get outta my fucking head! Grrrrrr!" Krueger gritted harder and scowled further. The Glock in his hand shook slightly. It was unsteady and at a dilemma that only its wielder could conclude. Marla's face took on the appearance of Krueger's wife. He started laughing psychotically

31

with his head tilted back. He suddenly snapped. He snarled and arched his eyebrows. "I'm not gonna kill you, bitch, but chu gon' learn tonight"

Krueger ran over to Marla and cracked her upside of the head, knocking her ass out cold. He then popped the trunk of his car and tossed her ass inside of it. Occasionally glancing over his shoulder, Krueger took the time to duct tape Marla's mouth, wrists and ankles. Once he was done, he tucked his gun and slammed the trunk shut on her. Afterwards, he ran around to the driver's door of his Crown Victoria and jumped in behind the wheel. He started that mothafucka up and peeled off down the alley.

Kruger drove back to his house where he parked into his backyard. He took Marla out of the trunk and opened the double doors that led down inside of the basement. He sat her down inside of the corner and shut the double doors, locking them up. Marla focused her eyes on him as he disappeared somewhere within the shadows to retrieve something. Not being able to see what he was doing, she looked around the basement. She was surrounded by a shit load of boxes and old furniture. Her eyes got as big as golf balls when they landed on a bone chilling sight. Sitting up at a dining room table, off to the side, was the dead, decaying bodies of a woman, a little boy and a one-year-old baby girl sitting up in a high-chair. They all had a bullet hole in their forehead. Their eyes were void of life and their mouths were hanging open.

"Mmmmmmm!" Marla screamed and screamed, but the duct tape over her mouth stopped the sound from escaping. She tried her best to get away, but her limbs being bound kept her immobile. She looked over her shoulder and found Krueger approaching her from out of the shadows, with a syringe in his hand. He grabbed Marla by the lower half of

her face and turned her head, sliding the needle into her neck and pushing the plunger down inch by inch until the contents of the syringe was gone. Once Krueger withdrew the syringe, Marla was out cold from the sedative he'd given her.

Krueger capped the syringe and placed it inside of his breast pocket. He then removed the duct tape from off of Marla and shackled her right wrist to the brick wall inside of the basement. When Marla finally awoke she found a twin mattress beside her and two bowls. One was filled with water and the other had two slices of bread and corn beef hash.

Marla stood to her feet, yanking on the chain of her shackle continuously. Seeing that the chain wouldn't give, she looked around for something that she could possibly pick the lock with but she couldn't find anything in the dim lighting that the light bulb inside of the basement provided. The only things she could make out was the dead family sitting at the dining room table and the few rats she saw scurrying across the ground.

At that moment, fear gripped Marla's heart like a pair of masculine hands. Her eyes were wide with terror and turmoil. She threw her head back screaming as loud as she could. "Somebody helllllllllllp! Helllllp meeeeee!!!!"

Marla screamed and screamed until her voice went hoarse and she fell asleep.

Tranay Adams

CHAPTER TWO
One year later

Krueger had this chick straight out of the Nickerson Garden projects running kilos of coke for him out of town for the past year. Shit was running smoothly until the last time he sent her off and she never came back with his money. He hollered at the nigga she was to make the drop with and he confirmed that they did business. That's when Kruger realized that the bitch had run off with his paper, and it left a sour taste in his mouth. This was the reason why when he sent the new twenty-five-year-old kid named Gerardo to make his first run for him he had the young nigga leave his younger brother, Valdez, behind as collateral. Krueger told Gerardo straight up that if he didn't come back with every dollar accounted for that he was going to slit his kid brother's throat from ear to ear.

So here the forty-five-year-old Krueger was sitting in the driver's seat of his Crown Victoria, gnawing on a toothpick and watching the rearview mirror, waiting for Gerardo to return. Krueger was a tall, White stud with messy hair and a wide muscular body. From his appearance, you would have thought he was always waking up, throwing on something and then running out of the house to get to wherever he was going. At the moment, he was dressed in a powder blue button down shirt with a tie loosely around his neck and a corduroy blazer with elbow patches on it.

While Krueger was watching the rearview mirror, the eighteen-year-old Valdez watched the back of his head from the backseat. Standing at five-foot-three and weighing one-hundred and forty-seven pounds, he was indeed the smallest and lightest Mexican anyone has ever seen. His hazel eyes and light complexion was due to his father being an Irish

Caucasian man. It was also the reason why his family nick named him Milk. Although he was a little guy, Valdez had a lot of heart, often finding himself facing men two and three times his size. When it came to hand to hand combat, he didn't turn down anything besides his collar.

"What the fuck is taking your brother so long, kid?" Krueger asked Valdez as he switched the toothpick to the other side of his mouth, using his lips to perform the action.

Valdez looked over his shoulder out of the back window of the automobile. When he didn't see Gerardo coming out of the doors of the building, he sat back down in his seat, saying, "I don't know. Maybe you should call 'em."

"Yeah, you're right. Brightest fucking idea you've had all night." Krueger flipped open his flip cellular with his thumb and searched for the number to the throwaway cell phone that he'd given Gerardo. He was just about to hit him up when Valdez told him he saw him emerging from out of the station. Krueger looked up into the rearview mirror and saw Gerardo walking towards them lugging a duffle bag. Right then, he shut his flip cellular and threw open the driver's door, hopping out. He made his way to the rear of the Crown Victoria and popped the trunk.

"It took you long enough." Krueger grabbed the duffle bag from him and dumped it inside of the trunk.

"Yeah, I know." Gerardo said before hopping into the front seat.

"Smart ass." Krueger slammed the trunk shut and made his way back over to the driver's door. When he hopped in behind the wheel, he found Gerardo and Valdez slapping hands and hugging, looking to be genuinely happy to see one another again. Once pleasantries were exchanged, the angry, White man didn't waste any time peeling from out of the parking lot.

Krueger parked the Crown Victoria and everyone hopped out. He snatched the duffle bag from out of the trunk and slammed it shut. The collective of men for the short gated fence of his house. Loitering out front was a couple of young knuckleheads drinking, blowing Kush and shooting the shit. Silence fell on their conversation once they saw Krueger approaching. They parted like the red sea and left a clear path to the gate. They may have talked shit about how they would air Krueger out behind his back, but the truth was not a soul out of the lot wanted a problem with him. Everybody and their baby momma knew just how Krueger gave it up. Any funk with him and bullets were going to be exchanged, not words. He didn't play that shit; he was about action and would leave a nigga with a tombstone in a hot minute.

Krueger made his way past the walls of bodies getting nods from some and mad dog stares from others. He ignored them all and went on about his business.

Once Gerardo and Valdez had entered the house behind Krueger, he shut the door behind them and locked it back.

"Y'all niggaz stay right here, man, I'll be right back."

Krueger told the brothers.

Gerardo and Valdez watched as Krueger flipped on a light switch beside the basement door before opening it. They watched as he headed down inside of the basement, hearing him loud talking someone. They figured it was a dog so they didn't pay it any mind. A minute later, Krueger was coming back up the staircase and shutting the door behind him. Using the hand that he held the duffle bag in, he motioned for the brothers to follow him inside of the kitchen. They obliged.

Upon entering the kitchen, Krueger dropped the duffle bag at the center of the table. He then searched through the cupboards and the cabinets, growing frustrated with each and every door he opened. Having grown agitated because he couldn't find what he was looking for, Krueger slammed the cabinet door shut. He placed his hand on his hip and brought his palm down his brunette hair as he thought for a second. Recalling something, he snapped his fingers and turned to Valdez.

"Valdez, look inside of the hallway closet and grab the money-counter for me." He told him. "It's at the top shelf of the closet, all of the way to the back."

"How come you can't get it yourself?" Valdez asked, with a frown. He was the youngest out of him and Gerardo and he hated anyone to boss him around, unless it was his big brother. He could accept orders from him because he'd been taking care of him since they'd been out in the streets, but anybody else he had a problem with.

"'Cause I'm telling you to, mothafucka," Krueger told him, eyebrows arched and nostrils flared. "So far I'm having an all right night, let's not fuck it up, okay?"

Gerardo wasn't feeling how Krueger was coming at his younger brother, but he wasn't about to get into it with him. The last thing he wanted to do was fuck up the money. It was too easy for Krueger to go get some other poor illegal immigrants to make his dope runs for him. With that in mind, Gerardo nudged Valdez and said, "Go ahead, Milk. The sooner business is done the sooner we're able to get outta here." He ruffled Valdez' head and patted him on the back.

Valdez left the kitchen scowling and talking shit under his breath. A moment later, he returned to the kitchen with an old, black money-counter. He smacked it down on the table beside the duffle bag and straddled a chair backwards.

"Thank you." *Krueger said and rolled his eyes like ghetto chicks do when they got a fucked up attitude. The only thing is his thank you sounded more like 'Fuck you'.*

Krueger reached inside of the duffle bag and grabbed a stack of crispy bills. He popped the rubber-band on the dead presidents and dropped it into the money-counter. He pressed a button on the money-counter and a green light came on. The money-counter beeped and began shuffling the money. Smiles emerged on Gerardo and Valdez' face as they watched the cash flicker through the money-counter. Although all of the money wasn't theirs, they were still getting paid for the move they made.

Krueger watched the money-counter attentively, smiling wickedly and rubbing his hands together greedily. Gerardo and Valdez could have sworn they saw dollar signs in his pupils, but they figured it must have been a figment of their imaginations.

Once the money-counter finished shuffling through the money, it beeped and a red light came on. Krueger was still smiling wickedly but when he looked closely the expression melted from his face. He looked hurt and shocked all at the same time. You would have thought that someone had told him his dog died. "What the fuck?"

Krueger shot to his feet and snatched the money from out of the money-counter.

Gerardo and Valdez exchanged glances.

"Krueger, what's wrong?" Gerardo asked concerned.

Krueger didn't hear Gerardo; his sole focus was on the Benjamin Franklin he held between both hands. His brows furrowed and he clenched his jaws so tight that you could see its skeletal bone structure. His face twitched and his nostrils flared. It wasn't Benjamin Franklin's face on the hundred dollar bill; it was Aretha Franklin's face on the bill.

Krueger threw the money aside and sent bills scattering through the air. He snatched up the duffle bag and turned it upside down, dumping its contents on the table. He quickly shifted through the bills, seeing that every last one of them wore Aretha Franklin's face.

While Krueger was shifting through the bills, Valdez picked up one of them. He was surprised at what he saw and understood Krueger being pissed off. Gerardo snatched the bill from out of Valdez' hand and looked over it. His eyes bulged and his mouth dropped open. He couldn't believe it.

"Raaaahhh!" Krueger roared like an angry lion and flipped over the table. His sudden mount of rage startled Gerardo and Valdez.

"Where the fuck is my money?" Krueger moved in on Gerardo.

Gerardo swept Valdez to her rear and slowly stepped backwards. She knew that Krueger could pop off at any moment and her body would act as a human shield to protect him.

"I'm sorry, Krueger." A mad dogging Gerardo spoke sincerely.

"Fuck a sorry!" Krueger barked, spittle flying from his lips. "Do you know what kind of shit I'm in? I'm dead without that money. And if I die, then I'm taken yo lil ass with me!" In one swift motion, Krueger snatched the Glock from its holster and pointed it at Gerardo's face. Krueger needed the money from the drop desperately. You see, he used to serve this twenty-two-year-old kid an eight-ball every two weeks. Well, one day the kid came short so Krueger wouldn't serve him his usual. The youngsta got mouthy and Krueger's hot headed ass popped him dead in his chest, killing him instantly. It turns out that the kid was the nephew of the capo of the Trombone crime family. And the capo,

Carmine Brasco, wanted three-hundred thousand dollars to present to his nephew's fiancé and baby girl. And if he didn't get that money, he was going to see to it that Krueger's black ass was pushing up daisies.

Gerardo held up a steak knife to him, he'd grabbed it from off the counter when he'd taken a step back from the brute.

"You brought a knife to a gun fight? You stupid, mothafucka!" Krueger's eyes bored into Gerardo's and his finger hugged the trigger.

Bloc!

Gerardo tackled Krueger and lifted his hand into the air, just as the Glock fired. The two of them fell up against the kitchen sink tussling over the Glock. Gerardo was putting up one hell of a fight but he was no match for the stronger man. Seeing that he wasn't going to beat him with raw power, Gerardo bared his teeth and sunk them into Krueger's wrist. He howled in pain and cracked him in the jaw. Blood sprayed the air. Krueger then kicked him straight in the chest and sent him sliding across the floor, bumping up against the refrigerator. Krueger moved in on Gerardo to finish him off. He went to level his Glock between his eyes and a growl came from his rear. He was just about to turn around when he felt a small body slam against his back. Then there was the blood curdling scream when he felt steak knives being jammed into each of his shoulders.

Krueger spun around in circles trying to yank Valdez off of his back. When he couldn't reach him he kicked off of the kitchen counter, sending him propelling backwards. The weight of Krueger's body came down upon Valdez's body and knocked the wind from out of him. The assault took the rest of the fight out of Valdez. Krueger clenched his teeth and threw his head back against Valdez's mouth, busting his grill and bloodying his teeth.

The smaller Valdez lay on the floor cupping his bloody mouth with both hands. Krueger slowly got to his feet and pulled the steak knives from out of his shoulders. He dropped the crimson stained knives to the floor and scanned the kitchen for his Glock.

"Looking for this?" a voice came from Krueger's rear. He spun around and found Marla pointing his Glock at him. Standing in the light of the kitchen, he took a real good look at her. She looked like a filthy cave women in her torn up raggedy clothing. To his surprise, she still had the shackle around her right wrist, which he concluded she must have somehow worked it from out of the wall.

"What do you think you're doing?" Krueger asked with menacing eyes and a heaving chest. Blood ran from the wounds in his shoulders and down his arms, dripping onto the floor. "Bitch, you not built for no bodies! I bet cha don't even have the balls to pull the..."

Bloc!

A bullet-skinned Krueger's cheek and a sliver of blood ran, dripping off the side of his face. His eyes were as wide as a fish's and his mouth hung open. He touched his cheek and his fingers came away bloody. Krueger mad dogged Marla and clenched his teeth. "You lil' bitch, I'm gonna take that gun and fuck you with it!" Krueger lunged at Marla and a bullet struck him high in the chest. He looked to the gaping hole as it trickled blood and then back up to Marla. He started for her, but staggered to the left, bumping into the kitchen counter. Feeling faint, Krueger went to grab the edge of the sink and winded up snagging the dish rack. He fell to the floor, bringing the dish rack along with him. Glasses and plates exploded into pieces, hitting the floor.

Marla kept the Glock on Krueger as she approached him with caution. She gave him two slight kicks and waited for movement. When he didn't budge she reasoned that he was dead and lowered the Glock to her side. Valdez came to stand beside Marla wiping his bleeding nose with his sweatshirt.

"Thank you." Valdez said to Marla.

"Thanks." Gerardo also told her. "I don't mean to be rude, but who are you."

"Marla." She introduced herself to the brothers and they did the same, shaking hands. She then told them how Krueger had kidnapped her and kept her locked inside of the basement, along with the rotten corpses of his family.

"I always knew something was up with him." Gerardo shook his head in disgust.

"Sick fucking bastard," Valdez looked at Krueger like the monster he was. "Is he dead?" Valdez asked. Gerardo nodded, having just checked the pulse in his neck. "Good, I hated that mothafucka!" he spit in Krueger's face and kicked him.

"Milk, take the floor rug outta the living room and bring it in here." Gerardo ordered. "We're gonna have to roll 'em up and find some place to bury 'em."

Valdez nodded and went off to do as instructed. Marla scrambled over to Krueger's body and began going through his pockets.

"What're you doing?"

"Seeing if he has some cash on 'em; ain't shit his dead ass can do with some money." Marla said as she continued to rifle through Krueger's pockets. She'd already gone through detox from being locked down in the basement for so long. But she was still dying to get herself a blast of crack rock. After having ran through Krueger's pockets and

coming up with 65 cents and a stick of gum, Marla convinced Gerardo to help her roll his buff body ass over. Marla drooled at the mouth seeing the thick bulge of the wallet in Krueger's back pocket. Hurriedly, she removed the wallet and cracked it open. A smile stretched across her face seeing that the wallet was loaded with Dead Presidents. Marla snatched the Benjamin Franklins' from out of the wallet, folded them up, and stuffed them into her bra. She was about to slip the wallet back into Krueger's back pocket when something caught her eye.

Marla opened the wallet and flipped through the pictures inside. There were a total of five in all, but it wasn't until she saw the last two that she began to feel sick. A shocked expression seized Marla's face and the color drained from her face. She placed a hand over her heart and extended the wallet into Gerardo's direction. Wondering what had gotten Marla so choked up; Gerardo took the wallet and flipped through the pictures inside. His flipping slowed once she saw the picture of a young Krueger in a black policeman's uniform and then the one of him in a cheap suit and tie having a couple of beers with a few detectives.

Gerardo's eyes bulged and his mouth hung open. He looked at Marla and said, "You just killed a cop."

Instantly, Marla gasped and she threw her hand over her mouth, tears danced in her eyes and she looked from Gerardo to Krueger's dead body. She'd just killed a cop and if she was ever caught she'd be facing the death penalty.

"Fuck, fuck, fuck, fuck," A crying Marla smacked her palm against her forehead as she paced the kitchen floor, Glock held at her side. "That's it. I'm gonna have to go on the fucking lamb. I killed a cop. That's a capital offense. They're gonna gas my skinny, Black ass. I'm done, I am fucking done. I'm finish."

"What's the matter?" Valdez dumped the rolled up rug on the kitchen floor. He had a frown fixed on his face as he was wondering what all the commotion was about.

"This piece of shit is a cop." Gerardo nodded to Krueger.

"Get the fuck outta here." Valdez said, looking back and forth between his brother and a dead ass Krueger.

"I'm as serious as a heart attack." Valdez assured him. He looked to Marla to find her sitting the Glock down on the kitchen counter and going through the kitchen cabinets. She found a bottle of Jack Daniel's which she took down and grabbed a glass. She filled the glass with ice cubes and filled it halfway with the dark liquor. She then took a sip of the alcohol and continued to pace the floor, worry written across her face. "This is very, very serious business here, bro. Bodying a cop, I don't even wanna begin to tell you how much trouble we're in. Even though he's a crooked cop, he's still a pinche cop."

"Alright, alright, everybody just calm down," Gerardo waved his hands. "Nothing is gonna change. We're just gonna bury this pig twice as deep. Instead of six feet, we'll do twelve so no one will ever find 'em. Now, come on. Y'all help me roll 'em up in this rug."

"Okay." Marla finished off her drink and sat her glass on the kitchen counter. She then proceeded to help Valdez and Gerardo roll Krueger up inside of the rug. Afterwards, Valdez peeked out of the curtains hanging over the windows to see if the knuckleheads were still outside. They were gone. Since the coast was clear, they carried the rug that held Krueger's dead body outside and dumped that bitch inside of the trunk of his own car. They then raced back inside of the apartment and wiped down everything they'd touched. Once they were done, they hurried back outside and jumped in the

car. *Gerardo hit up Walmart, grabbing a few shovels and two bags of lye. He then headed far out into the woods where they buried Krueger twelve feet deep in the ground. Once they were finished they were all covered in smudges of dirt, from their faces down to their sneakers.*

"Ooooh, thank you, thank you, thank you." Marla collided with Gerardo and wrapped her arms around him, kissing him all over his face. Surprise was written across his face as he hugged her with one arm. He felt her body began to tremble and he wrapped his other arm around her, hearing her weep, teardrops wetting the side of his face. A frown crept upon his face as he wondered what she was sobbing for. "What's wrong, ma? Why are you crying?"

"Gerardo, what's up, foo?" Valdez asked him concerned.

Gerardo shrugged and said, "I don't know. She just started crying once she gave me a hug."

"I'm...I'm sorry. It's just that...it's just that. I was trapped down inside of that basement for so long without any human contact, besides that monster." An emotional Marla continued to cry. "I was so scared and sick since I wasn't able to get any crack. The pain I experienced was nothing compared to the beatings and rapes I took from that...from that bastard. Aaaaah!" she broke down sobbing again, body trembled out of control.

"Shhhhh, there, there, everything is going to be all right. You hear me? No one is going to hurt chu. I'm here now and I'm going to take good care of you. Come on, I'ma take you back to the car." Gerardo scooped her into his arms and carried her off to the car, Valdez following along beside him.

"Bro, I have to know. Did you steal Krueger's money?" Valdez asked his older brother in a hushed tone.

There was silence for a time. It wasn't until Gerardo had strapped Marla into the backseat and gotten in behind the wheel that he had responded to his brother.

"I kept the money. I put it up inside of a locker back at the Greyhound station." Gerardo admitted. "We're gonna need every penny of it if we're gonna start buying our coke from Black Jesus." Driving now, Gerardo looked over at Valdez seeing a surprised look on his face. It was from this he felt like he was sad that they had winded up killing Krueger. "Don't feel bad about what has been done, Milk. We came to this country alone once momma and poppa died. We were just a couple of spic kids from across the Border, looking for the American Dream. Well, we found it, lil' brother. The money we use to buy this coca will bring it all to us. That's a promise. Are you with me?" he glanced back and forth between the windshield and Valdez, holding out his fist.

Valdez looked at him wearing a dead serious expression and said, "Si mon," dapping him up.

"I love you."

"I love you too, big bro."

Gerardo pulled Valdez' bald head down and kissed him on top of it. He then rubbed it playfully and turned on the radio. Al Green's "Let's Stay Together" came pumping out of the vehicle's speakers. As the music played, Gerardo glanced up into the rearview mirror, seeing Marla peacefully asleep. A smile spread across his face. It was at that moment that he knew that he was going to make her his wife and spend the rest of his life with her.

"I want chu to meet my husband. Is that all right?" Marla asked her daughter, holding her hands in hers, looking her in the eyes.

"Sure. I'd like that...mom." Yada smiled at her. "Mom. It feels good to say that. I haven't said that in a long time."

"Well, you'd better get used to it 'cause I'm gonna be around from now on."

"I should hope so."

"I promise." She kissed her on the forehead. She then turned to the limousine and knocked on the back passenger window, with her wedding band. As soon as she did that, the door on the opposite side of the limousine opened and Gerardo stepped out, making his way around the car and over to Yada and her mother. He took Yada's hand, kissed it and introduced himself.

"Pleasure to meet chu, Gerardo." Yada told him, then turned to her mother. "He's handsome, ma."

"I know. That's why I married him." Marla smiled.

"Why don't you all come inside of the mansion? We can fill each other in on our lives over something to eat."

"Sure."

"Okay. We can take your limo over, and save me that long walk."

"Hell, the ride can save us that long ass walk. Ladies first," Gerardo held open the back door for the ladies to get inside. Marla ducked inside and then Yada. He got in behind them, shutting the door behind himself.

The double gates of Yada's mansion opened and the Mercedes-Benz limousine drove on through, parking on the cobble stone driveway. Everyone hopped out, to find Jabar standing on the porch with his gun out at his side. Yada introduced him to her mother and stepfather and told them that he was her boyfriend. Jabar tucked his gun and shook Gerardo's hand. He then hugged Marla and pecked her on the cheek. Marla and Gerardo continued on inside the mansion where Yada promised them she'd make them something to eat.

Yada was on the heels of her parents, heading inside of the mansion when Jabar grabbed her by her arm, stopping her.

"Yo, I don't know what chu gon' tell 'em about our setup out here, but make sure you don't tell 'em the truth." Jabar warned.

"Nah, I've never kept secrets from my mother and I'm not about to now. When I tell her everything she'll understand. She was out in the streets, too, so she knows how my father got down. This arrangement won't come as a surprise to her. Trust me."

Jabar's eyes lingered on her for a while before he took a deep breath and released her arm. "Lil' mama, I hope you're right. The last thing I needa hear is some uppity pissing and moaning about how I got her baby into all of this street shit, ya feel me?"

"Yeah, I feel you. And you don't have anything to worry about." Yada caressed his cheek and then she kissed him. Turning to walk away, she made sure to grab the bulge in his pants before going on about her business.

"Alright now, don't start nothing while moms and nem here." Jabar said taking the Backwood from behind his ear and putting it into his mouth. He then fished a lighter from out of his pocket and fired up the blunt.

"Please, you ain't ready for this again." Yada capped, making sure to throw a little extra something, something into her step as she walked away. Jabar plucked the bleezy out of his mouth and made sure to watch her too.

Yada whipped up some spaghetti, fried chicken wings, garlic bread and a Caesar salad. All of which they had glasses of red wine with. For dessert she served Pecan pie which her mother and stepfather loved. Over dinner everyone filled each other in on their lives. Yada told her parents the whole truth and nothing but the truth, while Marla and Gerardo lied. Well, partially. They told the truth about how they had met, but left the part out about Marla having killed who she later found out was a cop. They then told her that they were rich because they were the CEOs of the third largest security firm in the United States. Yada was so happy for her mother upon hearing that, although it was all bullshit.

Marla and Gerardo talked and talked until they found themselves getting sleepy. They were about to take their two-hour drive home to Calabasas, but Yada insisted that they stay overnight inside of the guest room. Jabar wasn't feeling that but Yada didn't give a fuck. She finally had her mother home, and wanted to be around her for as long as she could. So with the decision having been made on Yada's part, Marla and Gerardo were staying the night in the guest room. They were given underclothes and pajamas to sleep in. and Yada showed them how to work the television inside of the guest room. Once she'd done this, Yada kissed her parents goodnight and shut the door to their bedroom.

**

Voss and Dough Boy sat at the kitchen table running dead faces through money-counting machines and separating them into twenty thousand dollar stacks. Once they'd crunched in the numbers in the calculator and wrote down digits, they'd go back to running the money through the money-counting machines. There were ten cardboard boxes surrounding the brothers' feet, all of which were loaded with cash. After a while, Dough Boy got tired of running money and crunching numbers. He dropped his pen down on the note pad and rose from off his chair. He threw his head back and stretched his arms, yawning and shit.

"Blood, I'm tired than a mothafucka, and I'm hungry." Dough Boy said as he leaned from left to right. He was looking at Voss who was still running loot through the money-counting machines and crunching numbers.

"We're almost done, fat man. Once we're done we can hit up whatever eat spot you want, my treat." Voss told him, keeping his eyes on what he was doing.

"Put that on something, Blood." He walked over to the black leather couch and picked up the remote control, turning on the 40-inch flat screen television that was mounted on the wall. He flipped through the channels until he found the movie *Taken*. He sat on the arm of the couch and started watching the screen.

"Onna set, P." Voss said continuing to crunch the numbers and scribble on his notepad. Once he finished, he grabbed his notepad and looked at it and then he grabbed Dough Boy's notepad. Voss looked between both notepads. He then sat them both down and started crunching numbers in his calculator. As his eyes got bigger and his mouth hung open, he slid the ink pen behind his ear, staring at the number that was across the small screen of the calculator. He leaned back on the hind legs of his iron chair. "Damn, my nigga, Sin City's the lick."

Dough Boy looked to his right-hand man and said, "Oh, yeah, what chu got?" he tossed the remote control aside and walked over to Voss, taking the calculator from him. He looked at the calculator and his eyes got as big as saucers. He whistled at the digits scrolled across the display. "Nigga, one point seven mill? Ooou, wee!" he said while holding his chubby fist to his mouth.

"Niggaz caked off that much loot, and only been down here a couple of months. You can't tell me that Vegas ain't where it's at."

"It most definitely is." Doughboy folded his arms across his chest and sat down on the edge of the kitchen table. "To think, you only came down here to get cho money up so you could lock ass with this bitch ass nigga Jabar."

Voss' face balled up and he gritted, clenching his fists so tight that his knuckles bulged. He shot up so fast from his chair that it fell over onto the floor. He walked over to the window and peered out of it, seeing the Bloods out of the corner of his eyes. They were posted just outside of the door with them choppaz, just in case a couple of fuck-niggaz wanted to try their luck and run up in the stash house, on some kamikaze shit. Voss wasn't staring at anything outside. He was more so thinking inside of his head.

"My baby, Blood, my sweet lady is locked up in that fucking mansion with that hoe ass nigga. The thought of her being with him drives me crazy. Them kissing, hugging, touching...fucking."

"Wait," Dough Boy approached him from behind. "You think Yada getting busy with dude behind yo back?"

Voss turned around to him and said, "I told lil' mama to do whatever she has to do to keep that bitch ass nigga'z suspicions off of her. 'Cause if he was to find out that she busted me up outta the House of Pain, there's no doubt in my mind he woulda nodded her." He threw up his hand which he'd formed into the shape of a gun.

"You sure you can live with that if she has been with 'em?" Dough Boy's forehead creased.

"Yeah, I got mad love for ma. She riding hard for a nig-ga, you feel me? A woman like Yada only comes around once every lifetime. I'm the luckiest man on earth to have her as mine." He claimed as he twisted his wedding band around his ring finger continuously.

"So, what's up, Blood? You tryna bring it to this fool soon or what? Let cho nigga know where yo head at."

Voss walked away from the window massaging his chin and thinking. Once he'd made up his mind, he turned around to his brother from another. "Fuck it. I gotta few mill now, let's do it. Let's get at this busta ass nigga."

"Fa sho." Dough Boy dapped up Voss and gave him a gangsta hug.

***

"Y'all like how I came to y'all city and let cha'll get mo money than you ever seen in yo lives?" Voss asked, looking around at all of the goons in attendance. The smell of Kush and Newports mingled in the air.

"Hell yeah." One Blood said.

"Niggaz really eating now." Another Blood said.

"Fa sho." A third Blood said.

"Good, good, good, I'm glad y'all loving this money we getting to. I'm glad y'all able to feed, clothe, and house yo families." Voss told them. "I gotta situation, my niggaz, and it acquires y'all help."

"Speak onnit, Blood. What's up with it?" Rampage said from within the audience.

"What's the prob, dawg?" one of the Blood inquired.

"What's popping, my nigga? Let us know what's up." A second Blood said.

"I got hella beef with this busta ass nigga back home in L.A." Voss looked around at the Bloods, seeing that he had their undivided attention while he was talking. "Nigga took my seat at the table that my old head left for me in his death, set me up for murder, and took my wife. Now, this nigga ain't no regular street nigga. Nah, I can't front. The mothafucka'z got enough guns and funds to take everybody here off their feet, families included. But I figure if we strike 'em hard and fast, he'll never see us coming and we'll have the upperhand. I'm sure I can fade this sucka ass nigga, but I'ma need y'all help. Are you niggaz with me or what?"

The audience went wild hollering and pledging their allegiance to Voss' cause. "Alright." Voss looked to Dough Boy and said, "Get them blowers, Blood, and make sure every homie got one."

Dough Boy nodded and ducked off inside of the hallway. A moment later he came walking back inside of the living room where all of the Bloods were at, cradling a cache of deadly weapons, ranging from automatic shotguns, AK-47s, M-4s, M-16s, etc. Dough Boy held out the pile of guns and the Bloods started snatching them up. Once those guns were gone, Dough Boy left and returned with more guns. Once those weapons were gone, he came back again, again and again, until every B-dawg in the apartment had a gun. Once they were all armed, Dough Boy came back toting a big ass brown box. He dropped that bitch in the center of the living room. Once the Bloods opened the box up, they found that it was loaded with ammunition for the bangaz that they had in their possession.

While the Bloods were busy loading up their respective guns and click clacking them shits, Voss ducked off inside of the hallway and disappeared inside of one of the bedrooms. Five minutes later, he came back out rocking a black beanie and a black long sleeve T-shirt which you could make out the outlining of a bulletproof underneath. Voss' hands were covered in black baseball gloves. He had the strap of a shotgun automatic slung over his shoulder and he was attaching a one-hundred round drum into the bottom of an AK-47. Once he'd accomplished this task, he called for the attention of the men he'd gathered in the living room for the night's mission.

"Y'all Damus ready?" Voss looked around at the Bloods.

"Yeahhhh!" they said in unison, pumping their respective weapons into the air.

"Alright then, let's go peel these niggaz' caps back!" Voss motioned for them to follow him with a wave of his AK-47 with the one-hundred round drum.

Tranay Adams

CHAPTER THREE

Vroom, vroom, vroom, vroom, vroom!
Black on black bulletproof Suburban trucks flew up the street, leaving debris in their wake. There were masked up niggaz riding on either side of the SUVs with machine guns, holding onto the inside of the truck. Dough Boy rode shotgun in the first Suburban strapped down with a bullet-proof vest and gripping an M-16. That nigga Voss was sitting on top of the truck with an AK-47 and an automatic shotgun.

"Alright, killaz, it's time to do some fucking killing!" Voss called out to the Bloods and pulled a red ski mask down over his face. He then stood upon the Suburban truck, deadly weapons in either hand. "Get ready, my niggaz, it's up ahead!" he nodded to the gates of Yada's mansion which was up ahead. Upon hearing this, the Bloods checked the ammunition in their guns and cocked them shits back. They then gripped them shits tighter, ready for a firefight.

Vroom, vroom, vroom, vroom, vroom!
The armored Suburban trucks looked like black blurs in the night they were speeding up the block so fucking fast. The gates of the mansion seemed to be getting closer and closer. Voss peered closer and aimed both of his weapons at the mothafucka chilling in the guard shack, just outside the gates of the mansion. The nigga had a goofy ass smile on his face so he figured he must have been talking to his bitch or something, hence the reason why a cell phone was glued to his ear. He dropped his cellular as soon as he saw Voss' Black ass on top of the Suburban though. He went to grab his AK-47, but by then, Voss was already lighting his ass on fire.

Bloom!

57

Fire roared from the barrel of Voss' automatic shotgun.

Blatatatatatatatatatatatat!

Voss' AK-47 joined in spitting hot flames with a vengeance.

The nigga inside of the guard shack spun around like a fucking ballerina as hot lead went in and out of him, splashing his blood inside of the guard shack, soiling the small window inside of it. When he finally went down, Voss could see the dead look written across his face as he sat slumped inside of the guard shack.

Ba-thoom!

The Suburban crashed through the double gates of the mansion, knocking them down flat on the ground. Right after, one by one, the bulletproof truck raced over the threshold and into the yard. As soon as they did, the goons on the roof of the mansion and on the ground who were armed with machine guns, starting busting at their asses. Voss and his Bloods were with the shits though because they started sending hot shit back at their asses. Niggaz was falling off of the roof bloody and shot full of holes, firing their machine guns into the air, freefalling to their deaths. Some of the ones on the ground were cut in half by the automatic gunfire, but not before giving fire back.

A lot of Voss' men were taking off their feet, and some of them niggaz lost a limb or two thanks to those high-powered assault rifles that Jabar's men had on deck. 'Aahhhhs' and 'Gahhhhhs' filled the air, loud enough to shatter a man's eardrums.

***

Yada got dressed for bed that night in her silk leopard printed pajamas with her initials on the breast pocket. She pulled her hair back into a ponytail and tangled a scrunchy around it. She gave herself a look inside of the mirror attached to her dresser, placing her hands on her hip and turning her head from side to side. Facing the mirror, she blew a kiss at it like Marilyn Monroe and walked over to her cordless, white telephone, snatching it up. Yada flopped down on the bed and dialed up LeLe once again. The line rung and rung and rung, until the voicemail picked up. Yada tried to call her best friend a few more times, but she ended up with the same results. Disappointed, she frowned up and tossed the cordless telephone onto the bed. She thought to herself as she sat her chin on her fist.

Something is up, Yada thought to herself. *This isn't like LeLe. We've never gon' a day without talking to one another since we've known each other. If I wasn't calling her then she was calling me. I'ma 'bouta get to the bottom of this shit. That nigga Jabar knows something and his ass sure as hell is gonna tell me. I swear 'fore God if he had ol' boy do something to my girl, I'ma splash his ass.*

Yada made her way out of her bedroom and down the hallway, slowing her stroll as she came upon a conversation between Tankhead and Jabar. She stopped at the beginning of the staircase and peered downward. She found Jabar slumped on the couch drinking a beer while Tankhead sat on the arm of the couch, facing Jabar, while he watched television. Tankhead was drinking a beer too.

"So what exactly did you do with the body?" Jabar asked, keeping his eyes on the flat screen as he talked.

"Man, I buried that mothafucka deep inside of the woods. Ain't nobody gon' ever find that bitch. On God." He took a swig of his beer.

"For yo sake they had better not. 'Cause if Yada ever finds out that you murdered LeLe there is gonna be hell to pay."

Instantly hot tears stung Yada's eyes and came running down her cheeks. She could literally feel her heart breaking into two pieces, right down the middle. Her soul quaked with emotional aching. She was hurt, devastated, and distraught. Her best friend had been murdered. She thought she had sent her out of state, away from harm, but she'd actually delivered her to the hands of death.

"I'm gonna miss you, girl." LeLe *swore with a shaky voice.*

"I'm gonna miss you too, Le. Where ever you go, I'll come to visit you every chance I get, okay?" Yada *said to her with a shaky voice too.*

"I love you."

"I love you too, mamas."

Yada *kissed her on the cheek and they hugged again, holding one another for what seemed like an eternity.*

Yada *kissed* LeLe *one more time before she released her, watching her get inside of Tankhead's car. As she watched them drive off, tears poured down her face. She wiped them away and waved goodbye to her best friend in the whole wide world.* LeLe, *still crying, hung halfway out of the passenger window and blew her bestie a kiss, smiling.*

Thinking about the night she'd sent her best friend off caused Yada to snap. Her eyebrows lowered and she snarled, speeding down the steps, screaming at the top of her lungs. "You mothafuuuuuuckaaaaaa!" she leaped over the guardrail and charged at Tankhead. He dropped his bottle of beer, hopped to his feet and pulled his gun from off his waistline. By the time he had pointed his gun to shoot it was already too late. Yada kick the gun out of his hand and sent it flying across the room and banging off the wall. She then kicked him square in his chest, sending him flying back, legs kicking wildly.

The nigga fell straight through the glass coffee table, sending an explosion of glass speckled with blood flying everywhere. Yada was so enraged she wasn't thinking when she grabbed a big shard of glass with her bare hand. In doing so, she sliced her hand slightly. She ignored the pain though and stabbed Tankhead in the shoulder. She then grabbed another shard and went to stab him again, but Jabar crept up behind her and broke his beer bottle over the back of her skull, sending suds of beer and broken green glass everywhere. Once Yada fell to the floor knocked out cold, Jabar pulled his gun from his waistline.

"You all right, my nigga?" Jabar switched hands with his gun and used his freehand to pull a wincing Tankhead upon his feet. He examined the shard lodged into his shoulder.

"I'll be okay, just pull this mothafucka out, G!" Tankhead grimaced looking at the blood running from his shoulder where the shard was still lodged. He watched as Jabar pulled the shard out of shoulder. He then ripped off the sleeve of his shirt and tied it around his shoulder to slow the bleeding.

"You good now, dawg. See, I told you there'd be hell to pay for capping ol' girl."

"Man, fuck that bitch." Tankhead said searching the floor for his gun. Once he found it, he walked over to Yada to give her a dome shot, but Jabar's ass stopped him.

"Nah, my nigga, she's all mine." Jabar smiled evilly as he feasted his eyes on a barely conscious Yada. "Do me a favor and lock the door to the guest room so her moms and her old man won't get out."

"I gotchu faded." Tankhead did exactly what he had commanded. Right then, they heard a loud ba-thoom like the gates of the mansion had been knocked down and then trampled over. Right after, there was a hell of a lot of gunfire and niggaz hollering from being wounded. Next, Rondo came over the walkie talkie telling Jabar that they were under attack.

"Shit, it must be the Mexicans," Jabar ran over to the living room closet. Opening it, he took out two Kevlar bulletproof vests. He strapped on his bulletproof and tossed Tankhead one. He then took out two M-16s, slinging one over his shoulder and tossing Tankhead one also. "Hold it down with 'em out front, I'ma hold it down in here."

Jabar sat a now conscious Yada in a chair and duct tape her wrists and ankles. While he was doing this, Tankhead was peering out through the curtains, seeing three helicopters hovering over the mansion grounds. Niggaz masked up in what looked like body armor and army fatigues were zip-lining down from out of the helicopters firing automatic weapons. They were cutting down Voss' Bloods and the niggaz on Jabar's side. It seemed as if out of nowhere, another faction had entered the fire fight.

Tankhead let the curtain fall over the window and took a few deep breaths to gas himself up to the carnage that was going on outside of the mansion doors. Once he figured he'd gotten himself in killer-mode, he rushed over to the double doors of the mansion and opened it. He then rushed outside and started firing at any and every one that wasn't on his side in the war.

Jabar ran over to the double doors and kicked those mothafuckaz closed. Walking back towards Yada who was mad dogging him, he could hear Gerardo and Marla banging on the guest room's door trying to get out and demanding that someone open the door to let them out.

"You fucking bastard, you fucking bastard! You said you'd leave her be, but you fucking lied! You gave Tank-head the order to kill her just as soon as she was outta my sight!" Yada cried and cried making an ugly ass face that directly reflected her heartbreak.

"I lied? You wanna call me a fucking liar? Bitch, you a liar too! Fuck you thought, you were playing me? I knew yo ass wasn't feeling me. I knew yo ass was telling me what I wanted to hear! I just went along with it. 'Cause my dumbass wanted to believe that you actually had feelings for me. But, nah, I knew that was bullshit once you slipped and called out Voss' name while we were getting it in. I knew right then that cho punk ass had busted him outta the House of Pain which was the reason why I was gon' whack yo bitch ass just as soon as mommy and daddy's ass left!"

Yada harped up a big nasty glob of phlegm and spit it in Jabar's face. His face balled up with anger and he lost it; Jabar wacked her across the head and face with the handle of his gun, splitting her cheek and leaving a bloody purplish bruise behind.

"Ho, you got me fucked up. Gon' disrespect a gangsta like me? Like me, bitch?" A furious Jabar pointed a finger to his chest. "Okay, okay, I'm teach cho ass. You know what I'ma do? I'ma light cho ol' gangsta ass on fire. That's what the fuck a nigga gon' do, show you how a real G gets down for mine." Jabar stormed out of the living room and headed into the kitchen.

Yada could hear the back door being opened. Right then, she thrashed around and struggled to get loose from the chair, but all she managed to do was topple the mothafucka and bump her head. The fall dazed her a bit but she was still coherent when Jabar returned with a dented, scarred up red gas can. He sat her back up in the chair and smacked her across the face viciously. The blow stung Yada's cheek and snapped her ass out of her fucking daze. Jabar wanted her to know exactly what was about to take place before he got right down to business.

"I'ma burn yo mothafucking ass alive, ho! Right mothafucking now, you think shit a game? Jabar got some games for yo ass!" He started splashing the clear flammable liquid on her shirt, lap and around her feet, leaving a trail down toward where he was standing. Once he was finished, he tossed the gas can aside and pulled out a Zippo lighter.

"Please, no, no, no, nooooooooooo!" Yada screamed and hollered, trying her damndest to get the fuck out of the chair, but the duct tape held her in place. The most she managed to do was rock the chair back and forth, which almost caused her to topple the chair that she was strapped in.

"Uhn, huh, not so tough now, or you, Mrs. Get Bad?" Jabar struck the ball of the lighter several times before he was finally able to get a bluish flame with a yellow tip to spring into the air. The flame moved from side to side for a moment before standing straight up, licking the air. Its light illuminated Jabar's face and he smiled wickedly, thinking of how the gasoline was going to send Yada's Black ass up in smoke once he tossed his lighter upon her.

Ba-thoom! Crash!

Voss crashed a Suburban through the double doors of the mansion, knocking over the furniture and shit inside of the living room. Unfortunately, Jabar was able to dive out of the path of the speeding vehicle. He tucked and rolled, just as the driver's door of the truck was swinging open and Voss was attempting to get out. Jabar came back up, pulling out his gun, taking aim.

Bloc, bloc, bloc!
The hot lead shattered the window of the driver's door and deflected off of the door. Voss had just swung the door into the path of the bullets to save himself from being fatally wounded. Grimacing, Voss peeked over the side of the door and returned fire, missing Jabar. The two gangstas had a firefight until they both eventually ran out of bullets.

"Shoot me the fair one, Blood!" Voss called out to him.

"You ain't saying nothing, nigga! What's happnin'?" Jabar peeled off his shirt, leaving himself bare chest. Voss removed his shirt and tossed that shit to the floor. The men engaged one another, fists up, ready to get it in. They circled one another, searching for a flaw in one another's technique.

Voss faked a left and followed up with a right, punching Jabar in his face and throwing his head back. Before Jabar knew it he was hit with another right, then another, then another. Voss faked a right again and tagged his ugly ass with a left, bloodying his nose and mouth. Jabar took a bunch of wild swings at him, and Voss ducked him. Coming back up, he punched him in the face a couple of more times and danced around him like a pro boxer, talking cash money shit.

"Yeahhhh. Uhn, huh, you done stepped yo ho ass into the lion's den, fuck nigga! You dealing with a beast! I'm 'bout to blast all ya fucking teeth out cha mouth, bitch!" Voss gritted and caught Jabar with a combination, leaving him wincing and blinking dizzily. Angry, Jabar balled up his face and rushed Voss, screaming at the top of his lungs.

"I'm gonna kill youuuuu!" Jabar raged, with his arms outstretched to grab Voss. Voss switched up his stance and used Jabar's momentum against him, lifting him up high into the air. Jabar came down hard, landing upside down on the edge of the hood of the Suburban and then falling down, wincing.

Voss walked over to Jabar and grabbed him by the back of his neck. He walked his punk ass over to the driver's door of the Suburban and placed his head into the doorway, slamming the door against it, hard as fuck several times. Once Jabar was barely conscious, Voss let him drop to the floor and dragged him to the center of the living room. He stood over his opponent breathing huskily. He then spit on his face and kicked him for good measure.

"Weak ass nigga, you shoulda never fucked with a G of my caliber," Voss snatched his shirt up and slipped it over his head, sliding his arms into the sleeves of it.

Right then, the Mexicans flooded the mansion with AK-47s, forming a half circle around Voss, Jabar and Yada. They aimed their automatic weapons at the threesome, and what was left of Voss' goons aimed their M-4s at them. Voss' goons knew that they were outnumbered so they lowered their AK-47s, seemingly accepting defeat.

Eyes big, mouths open, Voss and Yada looked around at all of the choppaz that were trained on them. They knew that there wasn't any way they were going to get out of the shit that they were in. Hell naw, it was going to take a miracle from God for them to get their Black asses out of this one. Right then, the Mexicans parted and a shapely person in a ski mask, black fatigues and body armor came walking through them, M-16 slung over his shoulder. He looked from Jabar, to Voss to, Yada. He then pointed his assault rifle at Yada. As soon as Voss seen what was about to happen, he slid into the path of the deadly weapon.

"Nah, fuck nigga, you take her, you gon' have to take me. Straight up." Voss tilted his head downward and mad dogged homie that had his M-16 pointed at his wife.

"So be it." The masked man said with threatening eyes.
"Nooooooo, wait!" Yada called out, garnering the gunmen's attention.

"What?" he responded, eyes locked with Voss'.

"I know what this is all about." Yada said. "When my father was alive, you had a peace treaty with him, right?"

"Correct."

"Well, that treaty was broken once a host of your men were killed. What if I was to give up the man that ordered those hits, would you take 'em in exchange for my husband and my lives?"

Yada stared at the masked up nigga that had his assault rifle trained on her man. Beads of sweat trickled down her face and slid down her neck. She swallowed the lump of nervousness that had formed inside of her throat, hoping to God that he'd agreed to let them slide in exchange for the nigga that had called the shot to have his men massacred.

"Yes."

"Okay. Good." She took a deep breath and nodded to the man, saying, "It's him. Jabar."

"Are you sure?"

"Positive. It was him that gave the go ahead to hit the corners where your men were slinging on."

"You fucking bitch, I'll kill you!" A snarling Jabar scrambled to his feet and charged at Yada. Before he could reach her, the masked up gunman, slammed the stock of his M-16 into his temple, dropping his ass. He lay on the floor moaning and groaning in pain, bleeding from the side of his head. At that moment, his assailant signaled one of his men forth. The man placed zip-ties around Jabar's wrists tightly and grabbed him underneath one of his arms. Another man came forth and grabbed him underneath his arm. Together, they drug him out of the mansion through the hole that was created by Voss crashing through it.

The man lowered his M-16 and slung its strap over his shoulder. He then unsheathed his bowie knife from off his thigh where it was strapped. A gleam swept up the length of the blade as he carried it over to Yada. She watched the man with the knife carefully, fearful that he might slash her throat. She tensed up and her heart thudded in her chest.

"Aye, what the fuck are you doing?" Voss asked, he went to go after the masked gunman, but the Mexicans turned their AK-47s on him, stopping him in his path. Mad dogging, he looked around at all of the men, knowing they would blow his Black ass away if he made another move.

The gunman with the knife stepped behind Yada and cut her free from the duct tape. He then pulled the silver tape from off of her and threw it to the floor.

"Thank you." Yada nodded to him.

"Don't mention it." The masked gunman said, pulling off his ski mask from off his head; revealing his identity. The masked gunman was Valdez. Gerardo's brother.

Boom, boom, ba-boom!

The double doors of the guest room flew open; Marla and Gerardo were standing in the doorway, guns in hand. Valdez and his men turned their guns on them, but lowered them once Gerardo stepped forward and they could see him clearly.

"Mommy," Yada rushed over to her mother and hugged her affectionately. She then looked up at her and asked her exactly what her role was in everything.

"Shhhhh," Marla held her finger to her lips, hushing her. "You'll know all you needa know later." She cupped her face and kissed her on the forehead. "I love you." She said, caressing the side of her face with her gloved hand.

After the exchange with her mother, Yada ran into Voss' arms. He hugged her and kissed her. He then held her at arm's length, looking into her eyes. "Are you okay?" he questioned with concern. She nodded. And at that moment he saw the tears pooling in her eyes. This worried him. He couldn't help wondering what was troubling her. "What's the matter, baby? Why are you crying?" he asked, seeing teardrops falling from her eyes.

"I'm sorry. I'ma month pregnant so I'm a bit emotional..." Yada confessed.

"Pregnant? You mean I'm gonna be a father?" Voss smiled at her happily.

"Yes." Yada wiped away the tears that dripped from the brims of her eyes. Voss then hugged her again, kissing her on the side of the face.

"Yo, Dough, you hear that my nigga? You're gonna be an unc..." Voss' face frowned up when he looked around and didn't see his right-hand man. He looked at Valdez and said, "Yo where the fuck is my nigga Dough?"

"I'm right here, P." Dough Boy said as he was ushered through the crowd of Gerardo's men at gunpoint. One of the armored up, fatigues wearing niggaz that came down from the helicopter was at his back with a handgun on him.

"You good?" Voss asked. Dough Boy nodded yes. "Where's Rampage?"

"I'm straight too, Blood." Rampage said from behind him. When he turned around he found him being held at gunpoint too with one of Gerardo's men behind him. "We lost a few homies but most of us are still standing."

"Alright," Voss said.

"You're a dead man, cocksucka!" Everyone's head snapped into the direction where Tankhead's voice bellowed from. When they looked they saw Tankhead lifting up a M-

16 to shoot Voss and Yada, and Rondo lifting his semi-automatic machine gun right behind him to take the same shot. Before those bastards could slaughter the married couple, another married couple, Marla and Gerardo, pointed their guns at them and pulled their triggers.

Bloc, bloc, bloc, bloc!

Poc, poc, poc, poc!

Tankhead and Rondo did a little dance on their feet before killing over on the floor. Marla and Gerardo lowered their guns one by one. Gerardo took a deep breath causing his shoulders to slump. He pulled Marla close and kissed her on her cheek.

Voss and Yada hugged each other tighter, staring down at the men that were just cut down trying to take their lives.

***

"Jefe, exactly where are we taking this foo to kill 'em?" the masked man behind the wheel of the van asked. He was speaking on the small walkie talkie attached to his shoulder.

"Drive that piece of shit out to the ranch! I'm not just gonna kill that fuck for coming at my daughter-in-law and endangering her unborn child, I'm gonna torture that fucking bastard until he begs us to kill 'em." Gerardo spoke from over the opposite end of the walkie talkie.

Jabar rode in the back of the van between two armored up, fatigue wearing, masked up men who took orders from Gerardo. His shifty eyes moved from left to right watching the men closely. One seemed to be lost in his thoughts while the other was texting some bitch on his iPhone X. An evil grin emerged across Jabar's lips because he knew that the odds were in his favor no matter how small the odds were. He still had a chance, and that's all he needed in his position.

While the masked men weren't paying attention, Jabar slipped a small pocket knife from out of the small pocket above the big pocket of his jeans. He unfolded the knife and its tip twinkled like a diamond.

With a grunt, Jabar slammed the side of his head against the masked men on his cellular ear, causing an eerie siren to sound off in his ear, and take him off his equilibrium. Right after, Jabar slit the other masked man's throat causing blood to spray out, while his eyes bulged. He gagged and coughed while holding his neck. Once he'd wounded the second masked man, Jabar leaped up front and drop the small pocket knife into the driver's throat, dragging it around to the other side. Blackish red blood flowed like a river out of the masked man behind the wheel's neck. Right thereafter, the van flipped over and slid down the street on its side, making sparks fly. Once the van finally stopped, Jabar slid open the door on the side of the van and climbed out. He jumped down into the street, looked both ways and then took off running down the block as fast as he could.

Back inside of the van, the masked man that was on the cell phone hit Gerardo up on the walkie talkie, telling him that Jabar had escaped before falling unconscious.

Eight months later

Yada was sitting up in a hospital bed with her bare feet in steel stirrups. The light above her head beat down on her form causing her to sweat as she was straining trying her damnedest to push out her son from her slick womb. Yada's face was shiny from perspiration and her hair was stringy and matted to her face. Veins rolled up her neck and forehead as her brows furrowed, dripping sweat. The slick goo covered, bloody head of her baby peeked out from her

middle. Voss stood beside her gripping her hand affectionately and giving her encouraging words as she struggled to
give the world what was going to be their first child.

"Come on. I can see his head now." He looked from her
to in between her legs. "Push! Push!"

"Arghhhhh!" Her eyelids squeezed shut and she hollered;
intensity measured on her face as she strained to force out
the baby.

"Okay, that's it, he's coming out. Keep at it now!" the
doctor ordered, sitting between her legs with his latex gloved
hands prepared to receive her baby. The doctor grabbed a
hold of the baby and pulled on him as he oozed from out of
his mother's womb.

"Waa, waa, waa, waa, waa, waa!" a bloody, slimy baby
hollered and hollered as he was pulled from between Yada's
thick legs. The doctor holding him with his latex gloved
hands, turned around to Voss, who was standing off to the
side. He was dressed up just like the doctor was. He had on
what looked like a bonnet, surgical mask, apron and gloves.
He nipped the umbilical cord and handed the scissors to one
of the nurses. He then handed the baby over to another one
of the nurses who Voss walked over to the sink with,
watching her wash the baby off. Once the baby had been
washed and rinsed, he was dressed in a black beanie with
Daddy's Lil' Soldier in red stitching. He was then wrapped
firmly in a blanket and placed into Voss' arms. The thug
looked down into his son's face, smiling.

"Babe, lemme see, bring 'em here." Yada smiled and
outstretched her hands toward the baby. She looked like
she'd been through hell and back. This was her first time
giving birth and it had pushed her to her limits. She was as
tired as a runaway slave.

"Let's go see, mommy, let's go see your mommy lil' man." Voss kissed his chin and brushed his nose against his as he headed over to his wife. He passed his son over to her and hovered around them, his arm outstretched over the back of the bed. The love was bleeding from his eyes as he looked between his son and his wife. It was at that moment that he realized that he didn't love anyone more than he loved them in the whole wide world. He kissed his baby boy again and then he and Yada kissed. At that moment, all hell broke loose.

Gunfire and screams of horror erupted just outside of the corridor. They were followed by the sounds of sneakers screeching as people fled for their lives. More gunshots went off, and the sound of people hitting the floor and being trampled over was overheard by the hospital staff inside of the room that Yada had given birth to the baby in, as well as Yada and Voss.

"What the fuck is going on out there?" Voss whipped around to the door, a frown fixed on his face. Fearing for the lives of his family, he grabbed one of the medical instruments that were sitting on a metal table on top of what looked like a blue paper towel. As he slowly crept towards the door of the room, it was suddenly kicked open. A masked man in a cheap suit ran inside with two .9mm handguns made of black plastic and gun metal. He shot Voss in the chest and dropped him, leaving him on the floor gasping for air.

"Oh, my God, nooooo, noooooo!" Yada screamed at the top of her lungs, causing her baby to scream his heart out. Her loud voice had scared the hell out of him.

The masked man then set his sights on the rest of the hospital staff occupying the room. They were all petrified and begging for their lives but he didn't give a mad ass fuck; they were getting it too.

Blocka, blocka, blocka, blocka!

Blocka, blocka, blocka, blocka!

The masked man stood over the dead bodies he'd created with his twin smoking guns, observing his handiwork. He tucked one of his guns inside of his waistline and lifted up his mask, revealing his identity.

"Remember me, bitch?" Jabar mad dogged Yada with pure, unadulterated hatred, eyes looking beady and red as he gritted. "You took my heart when you killed Bang, now I'ma take yours!"

Blocka!

Jabar shot her in the chest. He tried to take the baby out of her arms, but even with her aching wound she held on for dear life screaming for help, screaming for Voss to get up and help her. Voss was lying on the surface teetering between life and death though. Thanks to his wound the nigga wasn't good to nobody.

"Bitch, let 'em go, let 'em the fuck go!" Jabar gritted, trying his best to pry the baby from Yada's arms. A mother's love was stronger than anything he'd ever encountered though because she wasn't letting her child go. Right then, a second masked man in a cheap suit entered the room and pointed his gun at Yada's head. When she saw the gun in her face, her eyes got as big as golf balls and she released the baby, just as the second masked man fired a shot. The bullet ripped through the side of Yada's head sending a small river of blood spilling out.

Jabar tucked his other gun and cradled the baby against him. He turned to the second masked man and said, "Come on, Ronie, let's get the fuck outta here!"

Jabar pulled his mask back down over his face and he and Ronie took off running out of the room. A dazed, hurt and bleeding Yada tried to get out of bed and fell flat on her stomach wincing. She crawled as fast as she could out of the room and into the hallway where she saw frightened people running back and forth across her line of vision. Her vision came in and out as she looked ahead, seeing Jabar and Ronie hauling ass down the deserted hallway. She tried her best to crawl after them but they were moving so fast, grow smaller and smaller before her eyes.

"Noooo, nooooooo, nooooooo!" Tears burst from out of Yada's eyes and ran down her cheeks, dripping off of her chin. "Nooooo, my baby, my babyyyyy!" she outstretched her hand.

Tranay Adams

CHAPTER FOUR

"Haa! Haa! Haa! Haa! Haa! Haa!"

A masked up Jabar and Ronie hauled ass down the hallway, dress shoes screeching as they made their run. Their ties and the coattails of their suits' jackets ruffled as they ran. They were making their way towards the elevator doors with people running back and forth across them trying to get out of their way.

Jabar and Ronie made it to the elevator lobby with a crying baby. While they waited for the elevator to arrive on their floor, Jabar tried his best to quiet the baby down but he kept on crying.

"Drop your gun and put your hands in the air, asshole!" an authority voice boomed from Jabar and Ronie's back. They whipped around and found a fat, Black, balding sheriff with a receding hair line. His meaty hands were wrapped around a Glock 23 and he was poised to fire.

"Fuck you, we're not dropping shit! You drop it, or I'mma put one in this lil' nigga'z dome!" Jabar bellowed from behind his mask as he drew his handgun and pointed it at the crying baby's face.

"Fuck you!" the sheriff belted back.

"No, fuck you! You've got 'til the count of three, nigga! One, two..." Jabar commanded.

"Alright. Okay." The sheriff submitted and threw down his Glock, throwing his hands up in the air.

Blocka!

Ronie put one in that nigga'z brain and the elevator dinged as it arrived on the floor. Jabar and Ronie ran in and punched the L for the lobby floor. Just as the door was closing, more sheriffs came running with their handguns. They looked up to where the elevator was going and ran towards the staircase, heading down to the first floor/lobby.

Ding!

The doors of the elevator opened and Jabar and Ronie ran out, guns up. They ran dead smack into police cars that had just pulled up, and they didn't waste any time busting at them.

Pop, pop, pop, pop, pop, pop!

Blocka, blocka, blocka, blocka, blocka, blocka, blocka!

The glass windows of police cars exploded and so did their tires, police cars lowering to the ground. The cops hollered out in agony as they were met with hot bullets. They fell to their deaths and dropped their guns, lying in pools of their own blood.

Everything on the other side of the double electric doors of the hospital was quiet, except for the red and blue lights of the police cars which were spinning and wailing loudly. Broken glass, blood and dead bodies littered the ground and gun smoke rose in the air.

Urrrrrrrrrrk!

A old raggedy ass navy blue van skidded to a halt on the other side of the wailing police cars. The driver, a scrawny, Black dude wearing a plain baseball cap, black sunglasses and a blue bandana over the lower half of his face, stuck his head out of the window and motioned for them to come on.

"Y'all hurry up, man!" the driver called out from where he was.

"Come on." Jabar tapped Ronie and they made a run towards the van. Jabar pulled the door open and hopped inside. At this point and time, the sheriffs came spilling out of the staircase door. They looked left and then right, and seeing Jabar and Ronie at the van, they ran in their direction. They stopped at the police cars, kneeled before them and went to aim their guns. Before they could take aim, Ronie tucked his gun at the small of his back and picked up the machine gun that was lying on the floor of the van. He cocked that mothafucka and turned, spraying the clip.

Blatatatatatatatatatatatat!

The sheriffs' heads and chests exploded like rotten tomatoes being thrown at the ground. They grimaced and hollered out as they were wounded, toppling over onto the bullet riddled cops lying on the ground behind them.

***

Gerardo lay on top of Marla behind the nurses' stations desk, using his body as a human shield so his wife wouldn't be harmed. He tackled her to the floor as soon as the shot popped off. He didn't see exactly who it was that was shooting, but he did see two masked up niggaz in some cheap ass suits. Gerardo was a gangsta so he didn't fear death, but he did fear for the life of his lovely wife. He'd left his gun under the driver's seat of his whip because he couldn't get it inside of the hospital pass the metal detector. Now, he was kicking himself in the ass, because him doing that may cost them both their lives.

"Stay down here, baby. I'm gonna see what's going on." Gerardo said to his wife before kissing on the side of her head. He then grabbed one of the rolling stools behind the desk and slowly got to his bending knees, peeking over the desk. Right then, he saw the masked-up dudes running across his line of vision. He then heard them going back and forth with a cop, before shooting him and then hopping on the elevator. "I think they're gone, come on." He told Marla as he sat the rolling stool down and helped her up to her feet.

"I'll go check on Yada and Voss," Marla told him.

"Okay. Be careful…" Gerardo pulled out his cell phone to call his brother, Valdez. He knew that he was on his way up there and he didn't want him to run into those to gung-ho niggaz that had just finished shooting up the place.

"Oh, my God!" Marla hollered out.

Upon hearing his wife hollering, Gerardo, with his cell phone still glued to his ear, ran towards her voice. He found her in one of the hospital's doorway with Yada's bloody body in her arms. She was crying like a newborn baby and rocking her back and forth. Her teardrops splashed on her face. Yada blinked her eyelids rapidly and gasped for air. Her bloody hands clung to her mother.

"Jesus Christ," Gerardo looked at a bloody Yada gasping and clinging on for dear life. She was staring up at her mother trying to say something, but he couldn't quite understand what that was from where he was standing. So, he approached her, kneeling down to see what she was saying. "What, what is she saying?"

"The, the baby, the baby," Yada said just above a whisper.

"The baby, oh, my God! Gerardo check the room for the baby." Marla told him, tears dripping from her eyes as if they were a broken faucet. Her eyes were pink and her nose was red, snot threatening to drip from it.

When Gerardo walked into the room, he found a bleeding Voss pulling himself upon the bed. He was holding his chest and dripping blood everywhere. Gerardo stood where he was looking around at all of the dead bodies lying about in pools of blood. He tried to walk inside of the room and nearly slipped on the blood, cell phone still in hand. He caught himself as he continued into the room, looking around for the baby. When he didn't see the child, he became worried. He feared the worse was to come.

"Voss, Voss! Lemme help you!" Gerardo told him as he approached with a helping hand. As he approached Voss, he turned around with a pale, sweaty face holding his hand to red splatter on his chest. The nigga stumbled forward, struggling to keep himself upon his feet. He lost his balance and Gerardo caught him in his arms, helping him upon the same bed that Yada had been shot on. "What happened, what happened to the baby, Voss?"

"The masked men, the masked men took 'em...They stole 'em. I've gotta go get 'em. Help me, help me get my son back."

Voss pleaded with tears in his eyes, finding his vision growing blurrier by the minute.

"Shiiiiiit!" Gerardo said, speed dialing his brother, Valdez.

"What, what's going on?" Marla asked wiping her dripping eyes with the sleeve of her overcoat. She was still lying on the floor, holding her daughter in her arms, watching her fight for her life.

"The baby, Marla, those guys that shot up the place took the god damn baby!" Gerardo told her, cellular glued to his ear. "Hello, Mano, are you here? Look alive, two masked guys came up here shooting and snatched my step daughter's child. They should be..."

Poc, poc, poc, poc, poc, poc!

Bloc, bloc, bloc, bloc!

Blatatatatatatat!

Blatatatatatatat!

"Ahhhhhh!" Gerardo overheard Valdez screaming.

"Bitch ass nigga, come and get some, Blood!" he then heard Dough Boy's voice. "Aaahhhh!"

"Shit!" Gerardo ended the call and pocketed his cell phone. He then told Voss to stay strong and that he was about to try to get his son back.

"What's going on, Gerardo?" Marla asked, head on a swivel as Gerardo ran past her.

Gerardo stopped in the doorway and whipped his head around, saying, "I heard Valdez and Dough Boy downstairs, they're having a shootout with the guys that snatched up our grandson. I'm gonna go try and help them."

"Okay. I love you." She told him.

"I love you too." He took off running down the hallway. The dead sheriff was growing closer and closer to him the further he ran. He stopped in the hallway and grabbed his gun, checking the clip of the handgun to make sure it was loaded, before smacking it back in. He then kicked open the staircase door and stormed out of it.

Marla peeled herself away from Yada so that she could seek medical assistance for her and Voss. She ran down the hallway looking in every room that she came across, calling out for help.

"Help! Somebody help! I need your help!" Marla called out as loud as she could. "My daughter and my son-in-law have been shot! Please, somebody, anybody!"

Marla continued to run down the hallway announcing the same thing over and over again. Slowly, hospital staff began to emerge. One of them, a doctor, asked her where her daughter and son-in-law were located. She told him. A moment later, a couple of nurses, male and female, came out with two gurneys and two IV poles. They raced down the hallway, following behind Marla. When they reached the room that Yada and Voss were in, they were taken aback by all of the blood and dead bodies covering the floor. After pulling latex gloves over their hands and flexing their fingers in them, they worked together moving bodies aside so that they could get to Voss. They placed Voss on a gurney, tore his clothing off, and placed an oxygen mask over his nose and mouth. They then hooked his arm up to an IV and rushed him out of the room.

The hospital staff ran Voss down the hallway on the gurney shouting medical jargon at one another. Marla ran beside the gurney. She kissed Voss on the side of the head and told him that she loved him. She then told him that she would be back to check on him later because she had to go check on her daughter. With that having been said, she caressed and patted his hand before running off to see about Yada.

While Yada was being raced up the opposite hallway, a doctor held open her eyelids and shined a small light inside of them. He then turned her head to see where she'd been shot. She had a deep bloody gash that looked like a gunshot wound. But upon further examination, he discovered that the bullet that Jabar had fired at her had actually skinned the side of her head. It didn't enter her skull. *Thank God!*

One doctor slipped an oxygen mask over Yada's nose and mouth while in route while another cut her gown from off of her, revealing her bloody breast and the black bleeding holes inside of her chest.

"Okay, people what we originally thought was a gunshot wound to the right side of the head is actually a laceration that may have possibly fractured her skull. We also have a gunshot wound to the lower right side of the chest..." The doctor informed the staff as she examined Yada's body. She then went on and on with other medical terminology that you'd have to be in the medical field to understand.

"How is she? How is she doing?" Marla asked as tears poured down her face. She was peeking over the shoulders of doctors and nurses as they ran the gurney down the corridor, heading towards emergency surgery, to try and save her daughter's life.

"Ma'am, I'll make sure you're informed once we're done with her surgery. Right now, I'm going to need you to hang back and let us do our job, okay?" one of the doctors said as he held Marla at arm's length, looking into her face. He'd stopped momentarily to tend to her.

"Alright. Okay." Marla nodded as tears dripped from her eyes. She took a deep breath and shut her eyelids briefly, trying her damndest to gather her wits. Seeing that she was okay, the doctor continued alongside of the rest of the hospital staff, rushing Yada into emergency surgery.

"Oh, my God, Gerardo!" Marla suddenly remembered that her husband had gone downstairs. She took off running down the hallway and entered the door to the staircase.

Downstairs/in front of the hospital's entrance

Valdez and Dough Boy pulled into the parking lot of the hospital, nodding their heads to some Kendrick Lamar. They were in a black on black BMW 760 on stock rims. The two of them had grown closer over the course of Yada's pregnancy. Yada, Voss, Gerardo, Marla and them were kicking it hard as fuck. This made all of them become closer. Everyone became like a family with the strongest bond, and they wouldn't have it any other way.

Valdez found a parking space and backed his car in. They continued to nod their heads to the music while police cars pulled up out in front of the hospital building. The cops jumped out and got into a firefight with two masked up niggaz. This was taking place outside of Dough Boy's window, but like Valdez, his eyelids were shut and he was nodding his head. Once the song went off, Valdez snatched his key out of the ignition.

"Yo, that shit slap like a mothafucka, Blood!" Dough Boy said. He took a couple of puffs of the Backwood and passed it to Valdez. The nigga took a few hits and blew out smoke.

"I know, right? Kendrick the truth."

"Come on. Let's get outta here so we can see baby boy."

Dough Boy and Valdez jumped out of the car, slamming their doors shut. Valdez walked around his vehicle towards Dough Boy. His cell phone rung so he pulled that bitch out and looked at the screen. Seeing that it was his older brother hitting him up, he accepted the call and brought the cell phone to his ear.

"What's up, bro?" Valdez said into the cell phone.

"Mano, are you here?"

"Yeah, I'm here. What the fuck? Are you serious?"

Dough Boy at him frowned up. "What's up? What the matter?" he threw his head back, trying to see what was going down.

"Two masked up foos stole Yada and Voss' baby. My bro said they're coming down here any minute."

"Oh, shit that them, right there! They 'bouta get away." Dough Boy informed him and pulled out his gun. Valdez dropped his cell phone and pulled out his gun too. Him and

Dough Boy pointed their guns at the van, pulling triggers and popping off.

Poc, poc, poc, poc, poc, poc!

Bloc, bloc, bloc, bloc!

The driver's window shattered and broken glass rained down on the pavement. The driver ducked low and came back up with a machine gun. He tried to take a shot but Dough Boy and Valdez was on his ass sending a lot of heat his way, tattering the van. Jabar lay on the floor with the baby tucked to him alongside Ronie. Once Valdez and Dough Boy ejected the magazines from the bottom of their handguns, Ronie hopped out of the van and ran over to the opposite side of it. At this exact time, the driver was hopping out of the van, gripping his machine gun with two hands. They came to stand beside one another, weapons pointed at the opposition. Dough Boy and Valdez cocked their handguns and went to point them when they were suddenly lit up by rapid gunfire.

Blatatatatatatat!

Blatatatatatatat!

"Ahhhhhh!" Valdez screamed as a bullet struck his face and upper half. He dropped his gun and teetered from left to right real fast before falling to the ground.

"Bitch ass nigga, come and get some, Blood! Aaahhh!" Dough Boy's screamed aloud as bullets struck his chest and made him teetered from left to right, dropping his handgun. He then hit the ground right after Valdez did.

The driver and Ronie sprayed Dough Boy and Valdez' bodies once more before retreating back to the van, police car sirens filling the air as they rushed to the crime scene. Just as the van was pulling off, Gerardo was running outside with his handgun. Tears instantly filled his eyes and his heart sunk down into his stomach when he saw his younger brother, Valdez, lying in blood on the black pavement. His eyebrows arched and his nose scrunched up as he gripped his gun with both hands, chasing after the fleeing van.

Bloc, bloc, bloc, bloc, bloc!

Bullets whizzed through the air and shattered the back window of the van and its brake lights. Gerardo continued to chase after the van emptying his clip. But the harder he ran after it, the further the van got away, bending the corner out of the parking lot and speeding down the street.

Tires squealed back to back as police cars came to stops behind Gerardo. The cops piled out of their vehicles and drew their handguns on Gerardo. One of their voices came over the megaphone and instructed him. Gerardo did exact like he was told. He tossed his gun aside, placed his hands on the top of his head and got down on his knees. In this position, tears flowed from his pink, red webbed eyes and dripped off of his chin. He didn't give a fuck what the hell happened to him now. He'd just lost his younger brother so he was dead inside. So whatever punishment he got for discharging that firearm didn't matter to him. Whatever he got for it he was ready to accept it.

Marla burst through the staircase door and ran outside just in time to see Gerardo getting handcuffed.

"Oh, no, you've got the wrong person! It wasn't my husband that was involved in the shooting!" Marla cried with her hands over the lower half of her face, walking behind the cops as they handled Gerardo roughly, ushering him towards the back of the police car. As he was being deposited inside of the backseat, he looked up at Marla.

"Don't worry about anything, sweetheart. Everything is going to be fine." Gerardo assured her. "You get on the phone and call Goldberg for me. Make sure he gets down to the station tonight."

"Okay." Marla told him, looking at him behind the window of the police car.

"I love you." He told her sincerely.

"I love you, too." She told him back and sniffled, pulling out her cell phone. She then walked back towards the hospital, talking to Goldberg.

***

"That shit was wild, y'all! I mean, real wild!" the driver of the getaway van said to Jabar and Ronie as he sped through traffic, slowing down once he came upon a main street where other vehicles were. The last thing he wanted was to draw attention to himself and bring the heat of police. Lord knows if that shit was going to happen, then he and his niggaz were going to make the streets of Los Angeles look like that bank robbery scene from the movie, *Heat*.

"Yo, Tiki, shut the fuck up and drive this bitch, okay? I don't know who's louder, you or this crying ass baby." Jabar complained.

"Hold up," Ronie told him. He pulled a pacifier from the inside of his suit and passed it to Jabar who stuck it inside of the baby's mouth, silencing it. "See? There you go. The lil' nigga is quiet now."

"Yeah. Smart move, Ronie," A smiling Jabar dapped him up.

"Really? You giving me props?" Ronie smiled as he pointed a thumb at his chest. You see, Jabar and Ronie were both gangstaz, but Ronie was a little off. He was childlike in his behavior at times. When he was in high school, he was macking on some cheerleader after school and her jealous ex-boyfriend came up behind him and wacked him in the back of the skull with a fucking golf club. Jabar caught up with the fool a couple of days later and smoked his bitch ass while he was waiting for his food outside of a Tom's Jr. off of Florence and Hoover. Although Jabar got some get-back for his cousin, the injury he sustained left him fucked up for life.

"Yeah, I'm giving you props, kid. You did your thang out there tonight." He tapped him. "Matter of fact, I'mma give you yo favorite, a cherry Starburst candy." He pulled out a piece of the candy which was wrapped in a pink wrapper, handing it to Ronie.

Ronie's eyes got as big as saucers and his mouth dropped open as he took the candy, removing the wrapper as fast as he could. "Oh, boy, thanks a lot, cousin." He tossed the fruity candy inside of his mouth and began sucking and then chewing on it. He then pulled a Superman action figure out of his pocket and started playing with it. Jabar sat inside of the van watching his cousin play with his toy and chew on his candy.

Thirty minutes later

"Alright y'all, we're here now!" Tiki announced from the driver seat and started stripping down to the clothes he had underneath his suit. Once he was done, he tossed his disguise and his suit into the back of the van where Jabar and Ronie was. He then grabbed the red gas can that was sitting on the floor in front of the front passenger seat and jumped out of the van, slamming the door shut behind him. He whistled Dixie as he made his way around the van, splashing it with the flammable liquid housed inside of the red gas can.

"I'mma sit chu right here on that fool Tiki's pile of clothes while me and my cousin get dressed, lil' homie," Jabar said as he sat the baby down on Tiki's piles of clothes and started slipping off his suit. He was wearing a fresh pair of clothes underneath the suit. He dumped his suit in a pile and pulled off his dress shoes, tossing them into his pile of formal clothing. He then stuck his foot inside of a pair of Nike Cortez. Once he was done, he scooped up the baby and handed him to Ronie who was already dressed in the clothes he was rocking underneath his suit. The only thing is, he didn't have on his sneakers, and he was still wearing his dress shoes.

"Hold on, Ronie, you gotta put on yo sneakers." Jabar told him.

"Ahhh, come on, Cousin Jabar, I really like these shoes. They feel good on my feet." Ronie reasoned, looking down at his dress shoes happily.

"Nah, man, you've gotta toss them shits. We'll fuck around and get caught if you keep 'em. You know forensics are a bitch. And I'm not tryna get sent up state for nobody, you feel me?"

Jabar looked up at Ronie and saw that he was crying and his bottom lip was trembling. He took a deep breath and massaged the bridge of his nose, saying under his breath, "Lord, Jesus, what the fuck have I gotten myself into?" he then looked at Ronie. "Alright, check it out, how about I give you another cherry Starburst in exchange for you putting on your sneakers?"

"Yay!" Ronie jumped up and down happily.

"I'm running a fucking day care here."

Ronie placed his finger to his lips and said, "Shhhhh, Cousin Jabar, that's a bad word. Don't say that. That's not nice."

Jabar pulled off Ronie's dress shoes and placed his sneakers back upon his feet. As soon as he was done, he heard rapping at the double back doors of the van.

"It's time to roll, my niggaz!" Tiki announced from the other side of the double doors of the van. Jabar opened the double doors and he and Ronie jumped out onto the pavement. They looked around and discovered that they were parked in the alley between two shut down factories.

"I'll be right back, dawg. I'mma put them in the car." Jabar told Tiki to which he nodded and doused its insides with gasoline from the red gas can.

Jabar and Ronie jogged across the street to his old school Chevrolet. He opened the backdoor of the vehicle and let Ronie and the baby inside, slamming the door shut behind them. Jabar told Ronie to stay put with the baby through a hand gesture. He then jogged back across the street, holding his handgun behind his back. When he reached the van, Tiki was still dousing the inside of the van with gasoline.

"You almost done, big dawg?" Jabar asked as he stuck his head over Tiki's shoulder, leaning his hand up against the open door of the van.

"Yeah, matter of fact, I'm through." Tiki tilted the gas can upside down, emptying the last of its contents. He then tossed the gas can aside in the van and turned around. As soon as he did, he found himself staring down the black, hollow barrel of Jabar's handgun. His eyes nearly popped out of his head and he went to scream, but a bullet through his forehead, silenced him forever.

Blocka!

Pieces of brain fragments and skull flew out of the back of Tiki's head. He went to collapse to the asphalt, but Jabar caught him up under either of his arms. He hoisted Tiki's lifeless body inside of the van. He then tucked his handgun at the small of his back. Jabar pulled out a book of matches and tore out a match, striking it across the black strip of the book. The flame of the match hissed to life and he tossed it into the back of the van.

Frooosh!

The entire van became engulfed in flames as Jabar casually walked away. By the time he reached the driver's door of his ride and opened it, the van exploded and its passenger's door went flying across the air. The door landed hard on the ground burning.

"Cousin Jabar, where did Tiki go?" Ronie asked from the backseat where he was holding the baby. He looked over his shoulder and could see the cloud of fire rushing out of the alley into the street. He then turned back around and waited for Jabar to answer him.

"Well, our good friend Tiki decided to stay behind and take a dirty nap." Jabar adjusted the rearview mirror and saw the fire escaping into the streets.

"Ooooh, I think I'll take a nap once I watch *Tom & Jerry* when we get back home. Is that okay?"

"Fine by me, kid." He took the liberty to put a cigarette into his mouth and light it up.

"How much money are we looking at getting for getting the baby back to his real parents?" Ronie asked. You see, Jabar had told him that they were breaking into a fortress to steal a baby from his kidnappers and return him to his real parents. He informed him that if they gave the baby back to his paternal parents that they'd reward them with a lot of money. He knew that he couldn't have told him the truth because he wouldn't have went through with the plan. Although Ronie was a little touched in the head, he did comprehend some of what went on.

"When we get that baby back to his parents, we're looking at one million dollars apiece...easy. The kid's folks are loaded, and they're very generous. We've just gotta contact them."

"A million dollars apiece? That sounds like a lotta money." He tried to count the amount of money he'd get for giving the baby back to his parents, but became confused realizing he couldn't add the amount up on his fingers.

Jabar chuckled and shook his head, saying, "Let's put it this way, you'll have enough loot to buy yourself five truckloads of those Starburst you love so much."

"Really?" Ronie asked excitedly.

"Yeah, lil' nigga. Really," Jabar assured him.

"Goodie, goodie, goodie, goodie!" he pumped his fist toward the ceiling while holding the baby in his other arm.

Tranay Adams

CHAPTER FIVE

"Pop, pop, pop!"

Voss' face twitched and frowned up. His eyelids peeled open and he looked up, seeing a young man standing over him. The young man looked a lot like him except he was a shade darker. He was wearing white from head to toe, had on an L.A. fitted cap, square diamond earrings, a V-neck shirt and a gold necklace that held the bust of his mother, Yada.

"Who, who are you?" Voss frowned up as the young man grasped his hand and pulled him upon his feet.

"V.J." the young man told him, pulling his sagging white Levi 501 jeans further up on his ass.

"V.J.?" Voss' forehead creased as he tried to recall where he'd heard the name before.

"Yeah, pop. Your son," He smiled and showed a top row of shiny gold teeth.

A shocked expression came across Voss' face and he hugged his son, kissing him on the side of the head. Hot tears stung his eyes and threatened to fall, but he squeezed his eyelids shut tightly, making them disappear. He then held his son at arm's length, looking him over. The youngsta did look like him, but he could also see his mother in his face as well.

"Man, you grew up fast. How long has it been?" he turned around in a three-hundred-sixty turn trying to gather exactly where he was, but all he saw was whiteness around him, far and wide. He looked down at his clothes and he was wearing all white too. He had on a white button down, jeans and Air Force Ones. He then looked back up at his son, seeing his smiling face which made him look more like his mother than him at the moment.

"It hasn't been that long. I'm only talking to you at this ripe, eighteen years of age so I wouldn't scare you off. I mean, think about it, a newborn baby talking to you like this. It would freak you out." He smiled and licked his top row of gold teeth,

rubbing his jeweled hands together. He was now walking beside his father.

"Yeah, you're right. That shit woulda fucked me up." Voss cracked a grin as he strolled beside his son.

A serious expression crossed V.J.'s face as he held his hands behind his back, looking his father square in the eyes. "Onna more serious note, pop, you gotta go get back out there. This ho ass nigga Jabar done killed up I don't know how many people in the 'spital. Popped you, popped mom's and kidnapped me! I can't even front, I fear what that sick mothafucka will do to me as long as I'm in his possession. So, you gotta get back out there. You gotta get back home and put cho gangsta down on him and his punk ass homeboy! Show dem mothafuckaz that the Purdies aren't nothing to fuck with, you feel?"

A very serious looking Voss nodded his head, saying, "You're right, son. As soon as I get home, I'mma make 'em bow down to my gangsta. I'mma show 'em just how niggaz outta the Low Bottoms get down for theirs, nah what I'm saying?"

A smiling V.J. stopped and turned to his father, placing his hand on his shoulder. "See there? That's what I'm talking about, pop. Now go get 'em!"

"Clearrrr!" A nurse called out.

The doctor pressed the handled pads of the defibrillator to Voss' chest.

Boom!

His bare chest jerked violently from the electrical jolts sent through his heart. "Fuck, turn it up!" he called out over his shoulder then pressed the pads against Voss' chest again.

Boom!

Beeeeeeep!

The green line ran from both sides of the heart monitor, flat line.

"Come on, Voss!" the doctor spoke in a tone that only he and Voss could hear.

94

"Clearrrr!" a nurse yelled.

Boom!

Voss' body jerked again from the shock of the pads.

"Clear!"

Boom!

Besides the noise that the medical machines made, all was silent inside of the room. The doctor stood over Voss holding the handles of the pads. Chest rising and falling, as he stared down at him; his forehead beaded with sweat.

"Come on, come on, come on." He said again so only his patient could hear him. And then it happened...the green line started moving with a zig zag and beeping every so often.

Voss' eyelids peeled open; he took a breath, the first of many. Through hooded eyes his pupils moved about, seeing the blinding florescent lights above and making out the shapes of the hospital staff as they moved around him.

"He's back, we've got 'em!" the doctor yelled, smiling behind the surgical mask. All of the medical staff in the room started smiling. Some of them hugged one another, others high-fived while the rest did fists pumps.

Later that night

"VJayyyyyyyyy!" Voss shot up in bed reaching out for his son, but he was gone.

His face was shiny from perspiration and beads of sweat were on his forehead. He was wearing a hospital gown. He looked around the room. There were Get Well soon cards stapled to the wall at the back of him, a vase loaded with roses on his dresser alongside a portrait of him and a pregnant Yada. They were both naked as he stood behind her, holding her belly as she stared down at it smiling.

"Haa! Haa! Haa! Haa! Haa! Haa! Haa! Haa!"

His head slightly moved up and down as he huffed and puffed, wiping the sweat trickling from the corner of his brow.

He continued to look around, seeing the machinery that he was hooked up to beside his head. He lifted up his gown and saw the wounds from his gunshots had been patched up. He touched his face and it was clean shaven. He touched his head and it was braided into six frizzy cornrows.

"Yada!" his eyes came alive as he recalled his wife.

He started ripping the patches off of his body and taking the IV out of his arm. As soon as he did, the machine started beeping loudly. Voss threw the sheet from off of his body and went to step out of bed, falling hard on to the floor, busting his mouth. He peeled his face up from off the surface wincing. His mouth was bloody from the impact of the fall. He grabbed the edge of the bed and pulled himself up, almost falling again. Once he figured he'd gotten in control of his equilibrium, he made staggering steps to towards the door, seeing an over-weight nurse coming towards him from the nurses' check-in station. Her eyes were big and her mouth was wide with surprise. It was like she couldn't believe he was on his feet.

"Mr. Purdy, I'm glad to see you're up and on your feet. But I think it's best you lay back down. You're still weak from heavy sedation and your wou…" the nurse was cut short by Voss snatching his arm from her roughly.

She left him be and watched as he made his way down the hallway, holding onto the wall and calling after the love of his life, with tears in his eyes.

"Yada, Yada, Yada! Where are you, baby? Tell me where you are! I need you, baby! Come to me!" By this time, more of the hospital staff on that particular floor began to emerge, trying to see who it was calling out to someone. When they all came out, the overweight nurse exchanged words with them letting them know what was going on.

"Voss, Voss, Voss!" Yada called out from the opposite end of the hallway.

She emerged from out of her room pushing on an IV pole. Her head was wrapped in a bandage with a blood stain on it from where the bullet had skinned the side of her head. She was wearing a hospital issued gown. Yada wandered down the hallway, looking in each and every room that she came across, hoping to come across the only man in the world she loved with all of her heart.

Voss' head snapped around to where he'd heard the voice come from. When he looked and saw his wife, a weak smile came across his face and he turned around, making his way towards her.

"I'm right here, baby!" Voss told her, garnering her attention. He made his way toward her as fast as he could on his wobbling legs, trying his reach her quickly. His bottom lip trembled, and tears flooded his cheeks.

"Oh, my God, I thought I lost you forever!" Yada told him, bottom lip quivering, tears flooding her cheeks.

"I thought I lost you too. I love you so much!" Voss wrapped his arms around her, and she wrapped her arms around him.

"I love you so much, too." Yada confessed, kissing him long and hard as she cupped his face. They then dropped to their knees on the waxed floor, holding each other and sobbing their eyes out. They were happy that both of them were alive because they just knew within their hearts that they both were dead. But thank God for the miracle that they were experiencing right this minute. It all felt like a dream, but it was very well a reality… a reality that they never wanted to change.

"Voss, you're up? Yada, you're too." Marla came from out of Yada's room. She was using the restroom when Yada finally came to from her surgery. When she came out of the restroom Yada was gone.

"Mom," Yada broke her embrace from Voss and ran into the arms of her mother, holding her tightly. They held one another in each other's arms crying aloud. "Mom, when did you get here?"

"I've been here all day, going back and forth between you and Voss' rooms." Marla said as she pulled away from her daughter wiping the wetness from the corners of her eyes with her thumbs and index fingers.

"What's up with the Mexicans?" Voss asked Marla as she helped him to his feet. When he came out of his room, he noticed the Mexicans who were obviously members of BDOG posted up outside of his room as well as Yada's room.

"I ordered them there. It was for your protection. You know, in case something happens like it did last time. You never know, those bastards may have wanted to come back to finish you two off."

"Thanks, ma," Voss kissed Marla and hugged her lightly. He was still sore from his wounds and didn't want to chance hurting himself further. "I was expecting to see my nigga Dough up here when I came to though. Not saying that I'm not glad to see you or nothing. It's just that that's been my man for eons. Me and my ace been like this," he crossed his fingers. "You know how it is."

A saddened look crossed Marla's face and she bowed her head, fidgeting with her fingers. Voss approached her and placed his hand on her shoulder, concern written across his face. He had grown to love her like a mother, so he was wondering what was troubling her.

"I've got something I've gotta tell you, sweetheart." Marla said as she took Voss' hands into her and stared up into his eyes. She could tell by the expression his face that he already knew what was coming but it still didn't prepare him for it.

"What, what is it?" Voss' forehead creased with lines.

Marla took a deep breath and finally told him, with her voice cracking from her emotions, "Your friend Dough Boy and Valdez were murdered in a shootout with the men that kidnapped your son…"

Marla was cut short as Voss snatched away from her and approached a wall. Yada tried to go after him, but Marla grasped her and shook her head. She told her to give him some time to get a hold of the situation. Her and Yada watched as Voss banged his head against the wall and lightly punched it, saying, "No, no, no, no, no, no! Not him, not my nigga! This can't be happening! That's my mothafucking dawg! That's my mothafucking BROTHER!" Voss exploded with rage punching the wall until he busted his knuckles and stained it with blood. He then held onto the guardrail and started kicking the wall, over and over again. Tears poured down his face in buckets. He assaulted the wall until he dropped down to his hands and knees. His shoulders shuddered as big teardrops fell from his eyes and splashed on the floor. Looking downward, he saw his reflection and then Dough Boy's over his shoulder. He started sobbing louder and harder then, snot bubbling out of his nostrils, gagging on his own spit.

A crying Yada and Marla got down on their knees on either side of Voss and embraced him, crying along with him.

***

Voss stood beside his bed signing the discharge papers while the nurse stood before him. He was halfway dressed in a wife beater and black Levi 501 jeans which were sagging halfway off of his ass, exposing his boxer briefs. There was a beautiful view of the city in the background thanks to the large windows of his room. The sun shined through it on his back, bathing the upper half of him in warmth.

"Here you go," Voss finished signing the paperwork and handed the ink pen and paperwork over to the nurse. He then took his prescription slip from her and tucked it into his pocket. She told him she'd allow him to finish getting dressed while she went to get the wheelchair to roll him outside. Before she'd left the room, he put on the Kevlar bulletproof vest Marla had brought him and strapped it on. He then put his Champions sweatshirt on and cocked the .9mm handgun that Marla had brought him, tucking it into the front of his jeans. She was able to get it up there by slipping the security guard a stack. The guard knew that Voss and Yada were victims of the shooting that had taken place at the hospital so he understood Marla wanting to make sure Voss was strapped up.

"You sure you wanna check out now, sweetheart? It's really early, and your wounds haven't healed yet. I know they're still very tender and sore." Marla said as she stood off to the side, watching Voss get dressed so that they could leave.

"I'mma keep it one-hunnit witchu, ma," Voss began as he placed the rest of his things inside of the clear, plastic bag that the hospital had given him. "I don't got no god damn business leaving this hospital in my condition. But I'm not missing my main man's funeral, and I gotta find my son before that fucking maniac fucks around and does something to 'em. You feel me?" He went ahead and tied up the plastic bag. He then turned around to Marla. "If something was to happen to my lil' man, ma, I would just die. I would literally curl into a ball and die. So, I cannot allow that to happen. I've gotta get to 'em before it's too late."

"I understand." Marla nodded. She caressed his cheek and then kissed him on it.

"This is a breaking news report."

The reporter announced from the '30 flat screen television set mounted high up on the wall.

"The suspects responsible for the UCLA hospital massacre and kidnapping have been identified as twenty-seven-year-old, Jabar Lewis, and twenty-two-year-old, Ronan Percy…"

Jabar and Ronie's mug shots appeared on the screen. First, it showed the pictures with them facing the viewer. And the second set of mug shots were profile photos of them. It was from this angle that Voss could see the scar going over Ronie's eyebrow and the tattoo on his neck which were six AK-47 bullets.

The reporter then went on to tell how surveillance footage from nearby stores of where the shooting had taken place, showed Jabar and Ronie purchasing the disguises they wore at the shooting. One was a department store where they bought two cheap suits while the other was a costume store where they bought two Halloween masks. With this evidence, plus other information given to them, the detectives were able to put two and two together and come to the conclusion that Jabar and Ronie were the suspects in the massacre at the hospital.

"These two men are still at large and have a newborn child in their custody. They're considered armed and dangerous. At this time, a nationwide manhunt is on for the two. Stay tuned for an update."

"Them bitch ass niggaz better hope that The Ones catch up with 'em before I do." A scowling Voss turned off the television with the remote control and tossed it back upon the bed.

"Babe, did you see the broadcast?" Yada asked her husband as she entered his room, a clear plastic bag at her side with all of her belongings inside of it. She was fully dressed and ready to go home.

"Yeah, I just saw it, lover." Voss kissed her affectionately.

"Wait a minute, Yada, you're leaving the hospital early, too?" Marla frowned up.

"Yes, mommy, I know you didn't think I was going to miss Dough Boy's funeral, or be there in helping my man find the fools that kidnapped our son? There's no possible way you could have thought that because, had it been me, I know for a fact you wouldn't lie down and do nothing. You'd do whatever was within your power to guarantee that I was returned home safely." Marla took a deep breath and nodded, understanding where her daughter was coming from. She had to admit that she was right. "I'm glad you understand, ma." She said while she held her hands in hers and then gave her a kiss. She then turned back around to her husband. "We already knew one of them was Jabar's punk ass, but now we know who the other guy is."

"That's right, and we're gonna put the smash on 'em both for what they did. Mark my words, love, them niggaz are gonna pay. I promise." He tilted her chin up so that she'd be staring him in his eyes. He then went on to kiss her lovingly. "You ready to get the fuck outta here?"

"Yeah," Yada nodded.

"Alright then, let's get outta here." He grabbed her hand and heading out of the room, in search of the nurse with the wheelchair.

***

Voss, Yada and Marla sat in the bulletproof Suburban as they were chauffeured to the cemetery. An escort wearing a pearl helmet, tan shirt, brown pants and black leather boots led them on a motorcycle, while a long row of vehicles tailed behind them. As soon as the Suburban crossed the threshold of Inglewood cemetery, Voss found himself taking in all of the tombstones sticking up from the ground. He couldn't believe how many people had lost their lives. Life was crazy to him. It was like one minute you're hanging out with your homies talking, joking and laughing, full of life, and the next thing you know, you're dead, in the ground.

Voss had killed many people before and it didn't bother him a bit. But for some reason the cemetery was giving him the heebie jeebies. The hairs on the back of his neck stood up and he couldn't help feeling like something was scaling his skin so he smacked his hand, stinging it.

Yada looked at Voss with a furrowed brow, wondering what was going on with him. "What's the matter, bae?" she questioned with concern.

"Oh, it's nothing really. I felt something crawling on my hand. It must have been a fly or a mosquito." He told her.

"Oh," Yada said and snuggled back up against her man, wrapping her arm around his waist. "I love you, sweetheart."

"I know, lil' mama, and I love you too." He brushed her hair out of her face and kissed her on top of her head, rubbing his hand up and down her arm soothingly. He then focused his attention back outside of the passenger window. He could see Marla's reflection through it. She was grinning while staring at him and Yada. If he had to guess them being so affectionate reminded her of her and Gerardo when they were together, and she couldn't wait to be in his warm embrace again.

Before Voss knew it, the Suburban was coming to a stop and the chauffeur was hopping out and coming around to his door. He opened the backdoor and stood to the side, greeting all of them as they piled out of his enormous truck. As soon as Voss got out of the SUV, he noticed how beefed up the security team was that Gerardo has secured for them. They were all Mexican niggaz, dressed in black suits and wearing ear buds in their ear. If it wasn't for the BDOG tattoos on their neck, anyone on the outside looking in would have sworn that they were secret service agents, but that wasn't the case. Nah, these were a few gangsta ass niggaz dressed in attire for a funeral and they were packing. They had to be. They never knew when drama was going to pop off. Don't get it fucked up though. Voss didn't solely rely on Gerardo's goons for security. He had a few of the Blood homies from Las Vegas out that bitch and they were packing too. They were in formal wear though. Those hardcore, gun busting mothafuckaz weren't rocking a suit for anyone. They didn't give a fuck who it was.

Any and everybody that had love for Dough Boy and Valdez showed up to their funeral. The church was packed out like it was a concert going down that day. There wasn't a dry face in the place. There was a lot of sobbing, whining and yelling. Dough Boy's baby momma and his momma fainted, and an ambulance had been called to take them away. Everyone lined up in the aisle to pay their last respects to Dough Boy and Valdez whose coffins were lined up at the back of the church. The deceased had a closed coffin arrangement since the bullets had decimated their faces and upper bodies so all the mourners could do was say a few words and go on about their business.

Voss came up to Dough Boy's coffin, dressed in dark burgundy tinted shades and a matching suit. A burgundy bandana peeked out of the breast pocket of his suit's jacket. He placed his hand at the bottom of the sleek black coffin and glided it up to head of the coffin. He plucked his bandana out of his breast pocket and flapped it out, draping it over the center of Dough Boy's coffin. He then leaned downward and whispered, "I'mma get at them bitch ass niggaz that laid you down, loved one. Word is bond. Watch over me and mine until we clique up again. I loved you, my nigga, always have and I always will." He kissed the coffin and patted it before walking off, tears sliding down from beneath the lenses of his shades.

Yada approached her man, using her scarf to dab away his tears. She then hooked her arm within his and followed him to the front of the church, tears in her eyes. She had mad love for that nigga Dough Boy. He had become like a blood brother to her, so she was going to miss him dearly. "You all right, baby?" she looked up at her man, seeing the solemn look on his face.

"Keeping it a P-note, no I'm not. I'm really far from alright. And to tell you the truth, I won't be until I've splashed them busta ass niggaz that downed my boy and got my baby. You feel me?"

Yada nodded and said, "I feel you. And we're gonna get 'em, babe, both of 'em."

***

Marla sat on the metal stool with a big ass Mexican fool at her back. He was wearing a black tank top that boasted all of his tattoos, a couple of which broadcasted his allegiance to the Boss Dawg Outlaws Gang. He was there with the first lady of the clique acting as her bodyguard. That meant he wasn't going to let anything harm a hair on her pretty little chocolate head, no matter what. Although Marla wasn't feeling having a bodyguard with her twenty-four-seven, Gerardo insisted that she did. Once she figured that it was better safe than sorry, she reluctantly agreed to go along with her husband's orders.

A smile graced Marla's face when she saw the door open on the opposite side of the glass and the jumpsuit wearing inmates walk in. Leading the pack was her husband, Gerardo, smiling at her. He sat down on the stool before her and snatched up the telephone, placing it to his ear.

"How're you, queen?" Gerardo said with a grin. You would have thought that they were just on a dinner date and not in prison by the way he carried on. Even within the bowels of hell he still carried himself with an air of power. Any and everyone around him could tell that he was a boss. And, how couldn't they? Everything about him screamed the shit.

"I'm doing, okay, king, but I'd be doing a lot better if you were on the other side of this glass with me," She said with a saddened look on her face but still managed to muster up a smile.

"Well, you may be getting your wish pretty soon."

"Oh, really?" she puckered up with life.

"Yeah, the ballistics from that bullet they pulled out of that sheriff came back and it wasn't discharged from his gun, you know, the gun they were charging me with for murdering 'em?"

"Yeah."

"Well, I was looking at death row with his murder, but my attorney says that he got it lowered to unlawfully discharging a firearm in public."

"So, you're still looking at some time?" she said heartbroken.

"As it stands, I don't wanna get your hopes up, but he think he can get it thrown out and I'll end up doing something for community service."

"If Goldberg can get chu to walk away with something as lil' as community service that's a bad ass White boy in a suit.

I'm talking beast. Them folks can't fuck with 'em, that's for damn sure."

"Yeah, they can't fuck with my boy. The best in the business, and he better be with the six-hundred dollar and hour retainer he's on. My guy doesn't come cheap, but he's been worth every penny since I've started doing business with 'em." Marla's eyelids narrowed into slits and she leaned forward, trying to see something that was on Gerardo. His face frowned up and he said, "What, what do you see?"

"I see you have a new tattoo there, what's it say?" she inquired.

Gerardo pulled down the collar of his jumpsuit and said, "It's your name with a tiara over it." He showed her the ink on his neck.

"It's beautiful, baby. Look, I got yours too," she turned her head to the side and pulled back her braids, showing him that his name was inked on the side of her neck, with a crown over it.

"That's sexy, mamacita." He smiled.

"Thank you, papi chulo." She blushed.

Gerardo and Marla chopped it up some more before the corrections officer called for the visit to be over. They said their goodbyes and Gerardo told her he'd see her soon. They exchanged 'I love yous' and went their separate ways.

CHAPTER SIX

"Yo, Sharkesha, you tryna make some money?" Jabar called out to Sharkesha, who was heading to her house with her newborn baby and her four-year-old son. She looked over her shoulders at him.

"Hell yeah, a bitch broke as a joke. What chu got for me to do?" she called out from across the street.

He motioned her over and said, "Lemme holla at chu. I'll tell you all about it."

"Right now?"

"Yeah. Right now, I know you ain't doing shit!"

"Fuck you, nigga! You don't know what I be doing!" she looked between her two children trying to figure out if she should bring them with her or leave in the apartment by themselves until she came back. If she knew anything about that nigga Jabar he liked to fuck and he'd more than likely proposition her for some ass. She wasn't trying to be fucking any dusty ass niggaz in front of her kids because she didn't get down like that. But she was flat broke so she said fuck it. If push came to shove, she could just lock the kids in one of his other bedrooms or something if he was trying to get busy.

"Come on, Ju Ju." Sharkesha said to her four-year-old son while she pushed her newborn baby in a stroller.

When Sharkesha came inside of the house, she found Ronie sitting on the couch holding a crying bundled up baby, watching cartoons. Sharkesha rolled her baby before the television and placed her four-year-old son beside her stroller. She then walked over to Jabar, who had his back to her while he opened up four baby bottles. When he felt her at the back of him, he turned around to her, looking her over. Sharkesha was a portly chick with big black and gold dookie braids. She had big ass titties that looked like they weighed half as much as her body did and a great, big old ass that you could sit a lamp on. She was fairly attractive in the face, but her hood rat attitude and lifestyle could turn a nigga off if he demanded more in his woman.

"So, what chu want, fool?" Sharkesha asked as she chewed gum and twirled her braid around her manicured finger. She had one hand on her hip and she stood with her weight on her left foot.

"I need some milk for this crying ass baby." Jabar informed her. "I give you fifty bucks if you fill up all four of these bottles with yo titty milk."

"Ewww, why you want me to do that? You sho' his momma would be all right with that? I know I wouldn't want the next bitch's titty milk in my baby's stomach." She said as she continued to play with her hair and stare at her nails, noticing one of them was broke. "Aww, fuck, look at my fucking nail!" her face frowned up. "But, yeah, you could just run up to the store and get chu some Enfamil formula for 'em."

"Look, just lemme slide you the fifty for some of yo breast milk, damn!" Jabar frowned up as he rifled through the wad of money in his hands. If there was one thing he hated it was a mouthful mothafucka. They got on his god damn nerves.

"Unh unh, nigga, what's up?" Sharkesha folded her arms across her breasts. "Why you pushing so hard for me to give you some of my milk, when you could easily just go to the store to get chu some?"

"I just don't feel like running up to the store right now, all right? A nigga been running around all day, and I'm tired as a runaway slave. You feel me?" Jabar was lying like a mothafucka. He wasn't trying to leave the house until the heat from the massacre died down. The last thing he wanted was to get caught up out there in the streets.

"Okay," she popped her gum and said, "Now, who baby is that?"

"Who baby is that? Are you seriously that fucking nosey? It's mine okay? His momma just dropped him on my door step with a letter saying she tired of 'em and that's it's my turn to take care of 'em. So here I am, asking my next-door neighbor to sling me some titty milk so I can feed 'em. Now, are you gon' gimme some of yo," he snatched up one of the baby bottles and smacked it down on the kitchen table before Sharkesha. "god damn breast milk, or not? Shit! Girl, you like to drive a nigga up the fucking wall with these hunnit fucking questions."

"I want a hunnit dollars."

Jabar's face balled up and he looked at Sharkesha as if she had lost her god damn mind. "You want what?"

"You heard me, nigga, I want a hunnit dollars for my mothafucking breast milk. Take it or leave it."

"I cannot believe this shit. Bitch is robbing me without the gun," Jabar counted off fifty more dollars and passed it to Sharkesha along with the other fifty dollars he had.

"Uhn huh, without the gun, so give it up, big daddy." Sharkesha rubbed her thumb and index finger together, signaling money. She took the money from Jabar and licked her thumb, counting it up. Seeing that all of her dough was there, she folded up the money and stuffed it inside of her bra. She then gathered the other three baby bottles and sat them on the table, telling Jabar. "Y'all fools watch my baby, I'll be right back. I gotta run home and get the breast pump; it'll make the job much easier."

"Alright," Jabar said, plopping down in the chair at the table and examining one of the empty baby bottles. He looked over from the baby bottle and spotted Ronie staring at Sharkesha's big old booty rocking from left to right as she sauntered across the living room floor, heading towards the front door. A smile spread across Jabar's lips looking at his cousin.

I'mma get that young nigga some pussy. It's about time he get his cherry popped, Jabar thought as he continued to toy with the baby bottle.

Sharkesha returned to the kitchen table with the breast pump. She sat at the table and filled all four of the bottles. Jabar watched her the entire time. Seeing the pump suck the milk from out of Sharkesha's breasts had Jabar's dick as hard as a diamond. He found himself tugging on his dick through his jeans, staring at her big, long breasts the entire time. She looked up at him cracking a smile and sucking the breast milk from off her fingers, trying her best to entice him.

"How much for the full ride?" Jabar whispered across the table.

"Two hunnit." Sharkesha whispered back with two fingers.

"For both of us?"

"Both of us?" she looked confused. She looked at Ronie to see him still watching cartoons with her kids. That's when it dawned on her that Jabar meant for him and his cousin to fuck her she was charging him two-hundred dollars.

"Nah, four."

"Unh unh."

"Okay, okay, two-fifty. But I ain't going any lower than that. This pussy is not on the value menu, baby." She rose from the table and walked over to the sink, turning on the faucet. She lathered her hands with Dawn dishwashing liquid and rinsed them off. While she was doing this, Jabar came behind her and slid two-hundred and fifty dollars inside of her bra. He then pulled her sweatpants and panties down around her knees causing her to bend over. She looked back at him as he unzipped his jeans and pulled his meat out through his zipper hole, shaking her big old bodacious ass.

The enormous brown orbs bounced up and down as she popped her ass. The sight of it made Jabar's dick grow harder and harder until his shit had curled like a bicep. He ripped the gold foil from off his latex Magnum with his teeth and pulled it down over his rock-hard dick. He then pressed his hand down against the upper half of her back, held her ass cheeks spread apart while looking down at her brown eyes and eased his dick inside of her warm, gushy hole. Her eyelids closed tightly and she licked her lips, feeling him fill her void.

"Mmmmm," Sharkesha said and then she gasped. "There you go, big daddy, gon' get cho self a lil' something, something."

Jabar grabbed hold of Sharkesha's braids and pulled her hair back, as he jammed himself in and out of her, making her ass clap like a pair of hands. While he fucked her from the back, he'd talk shit in a hushed tone and occasionally smack her on her ass sending a ripple up them.

"Unh, god damn you got some bomb ass pussy." Jabar said as he gripped her braids tighter, pummeling her from the back, watching the back of her head jut up and down from the repeated impact of his pelvis. While Sharkesha was enjoying the dick, Jabar looked over his shoulder, to find the children occupied by the cartoons. Ronie was playing with the baby and watching cartoons too. It seemed as if they television had everyone's undivided attention. As long as it was on they were tuned in.

"Fuck me, big daddy, fuck me!" Sharkesha whined as she was hunched from the back and her ass was smacked viciously. She liked that kinky shit.

"Throw that big mothafucka back!" Jabar put his fists on his hip and looked down at Sharkesha pump her ass back and forth onto his dick. Looking down, he let a thin river of hot saliva flow from between his lips and onto his dick as it went in and out of her pussy, lubricating himself. Once he got tired of Sharkesha throwing it back against him, he spread her big ass, ass cheeks a part and stroked her fast and furiously. He was piping her out so good that she stood up on her toes and arched her back further, enjoying the sensation that his dick brought her. "Where you want it? I'm 'bouta bust."

"On my, on my face!" she said in a hushed tone.

"Okay. Here I come," Jabar pulled out of Sharkesha and she got down on her knees. He pulled the latex off of his meat and held his dick to the side of her face, pumping it up and down. Shortly, hot pearly, semen oozed and shot out of his peehole.

Jabar rubbed his dick against the side of Sharkesha's face and then she stuck it inside of her mouth, sucking him off while staring up into his eyes. She made humming sounds as she sucked and slurped on him. Her skilled head game had him shut his eyelids and throw his head back, licking his lips.

"Damn, lil' mama, you the truth." Jabar looked down at Sharkesha as she continued to suck on him. A minute later she was popping him out of her mouth and rising to her feet, pulling her panties back upon her. She snatched a few paper towels off of the roll and wiped off her face. Jabar came behind her, grabbing a few paper towels and wiping off his pubic hairs and dick.

"Aye, what're you guys doing?" Ronie asked as he entered the kitchen, holding the baby.

"Nothing. Gemme lil' man," Jabar said as he took the baby. He then looked Ronie up and down, straightening out his shirt. He hoped that he was doing the right thing by setting him up to get some ass. The way he saw it, anything could go wrong after the stunt they just pulled and he didn't want his cousin to die a virgin. "Yo, you tryna fuck something?"

"Cousin Jabar, stop cussing. And what does that mean, huh?" Ronie's face frowned up. He didn't have a clue of what Jabar was talking about.

"Do you want some pussy?" he asked him straight up.

"Pussy, what's pussy?" Ronie's face frowned up further.

"You're about to find out, baby boy." Sharkesha grabbed Ronie by his hand and led him inside of the bedroom, closing the door shut behind him. Once they were out of his sight, Jabar sat on the couch with the baby and watched cartoons with the rest of the children.

Ten minutes later, Sharkesha walked out of the bedroom with an amused expression on her face. Ronie was coming out of the bedroom behind her smiling goofily. Sharkesha kissed him on his cheek, gathered her children and left.

"Welcome to manhood, my friend." Jabar hung his arm around Jabar's neck and walked him inside of the kitchen where he opened the refrigerator. He grabbed two bottles of Heineken and popped the lids off of both of them with a metal bottle-opener. He passed one of the bottles to Ronie. "This is cause for a celebration." He held up his bottle and so did Ronie. "To getting some!"

"To getting some!" Ronie clinked his bottle with Jabar's bottle. They both swigged from the bottles, but Ronie spit out his beer. "Ewwww, this taste like cold pee!"

Jabar doubled over laughing his ass off.

One week later

Jabar stepped outside of the back door and wandered around the backyard, lighting up a cigarette. He would have sparked up inside, but he was mindful of the baby. Well, that and Ronie constantly reminding him that it was bad for the baby's health for him to smoke around it. Jabar tilted his head back and blew out a cloud of smoke. Something at the corner of his eye caught his attention. He climbed upon the fence and could see through the kitchen window, straight into the living room. His perverted ass was hoping to catch a glimpse of Sharkesha walking around the house naked or something. But instead he found her sitting before the television set, watching the news.

A news report about the massacre and the shootout at UCLA hospital came on the television screen while Sharkesha was sitting on the couch breastfeeding her newborn baby. A shocked expression came over her face when she saw a picture of the baby come on the television's screen.

"Oh, my God, that's the same baby that was over that nigga Jabar's house..." Sharkesha said with utter surprised.

Jabar jumped down from the fence and returned to the house, coming in through the backdoor. He went inside of his bedroom and lifted the mattress, grabbing the .38 special. He carried the small revolver inside of the kitchen and stuck a potato on the end of its barrel. He then walked inside of the living room where Ronie was holding the baby and watching *Tom & Jerry* on Cartoon Network.

"Ronie," Jabar called for his cousin's attention. When he looked at him, he went on with what he had to say. "Lay lil' dude down for a minute. I need you to go next door and see if Sharkesha has some sugar you can borrow."

"Sugar? What're you making, Cousin Jabar, a cake?" Ronie asked intrigued.

"Yeah, a fucking cake, now go see if that hood rat has any sugar for me, please." Jabar said with attitude, sneering. He was annoyed with Ronie, but what was he going to do? The young nigga couldn't help how he was.

"You cussed again, that's not nice."

"I know. Look, I'm sorry. Could you go see if she has any sugar we could borrow, please?" he said nicer than he did before.

"Okay. But only because you asked nicely." Ronie propped the baby up against the corner of the couch so it could be sitting up to see the television. He then left out of the house and headed next door to Sharkesha's place. As soon as he was gone, Jabar crept out of the back door and hopped the short gate into Sharkesha's yard. He then hustled up the short steps of the back porch and picked the lock of the backdoor. Once the door clicked open, he made his way inside with the stealth of a cat burglar and entered the kitchen. From where he was, he could see the back of Sharkesha as she stood at the door talking to Ronie, voice a little shaky with emotion. She was afraid.

Sharkesha closed the door and made her way inside of the kitchen. Jabar hid beside the door, clutching his .38 special with the potato on its barrel. He watched as Sharkesha searched the cabinets for sugar. Once she found it, she brought it down and turned around, coming face to face with the butt of the potato.

114

Jabar's scowling face was right behind it. His eyes were unforgiving. Sharkesha went to scream, but before the sound could escape her lips the potato exploded and so did her forehead. Sharkesha dropped to the kitchen floor still holding her baby to her breast, telephone sliding across the surface. The baby hollered and hollered until Jabar picked him up. He rocked him to sleep as he walked back up to the front door, opening it up.

"Go back home, Ronie." Jabar told him.

"Wait, what about the sugar?" Ronie asked seriously.

"The bitch ain't got no more, man. Now, take yo ass home. And so what if I cussed, nigga, I'm grown. Now gone now, get!" he shut the door in his face and headed to the master bedroom where he smothered the baby to death. Afterwards, he entered the other bedroom and did the same to the four-year-old child.

***

Ronie sat on the commode while Jabar stood over him, applying a thick nappy beard to the lower half of his face and a cornrow wig to his head. For good measure, he slid a pair of glasses onto his face. He then motioned for him to rise from the commode, ushering him to stand in the medicine cabinet mirror. As Ronie looked himself over in his reflection, Jabar stood behind him, looking him over as well.

"Whoaaa! What happened to my face?" Ronie's eyes got big and he touched his face like he couldn't feel it.

Jabar chuckled and said, "You good, cuzzo. I just put chu onna disguise. I don't want anyone noticing you while you're at the store."

"Oh, okay. Why am I wearing a disguise again?" he looked up at him.

"Well, we haven't gotten the baby back to his rightful parents yet, so the fake parents are tryna get 'em back. If they recognize you, they'll kidnap you and torture you 'til you tell 'em where the baby is. We cannot allow that to happen." Once again, Jabar found himself lying to his cousin. The truth was that he saw the same news report that Voss saw when he was preparing to leave the hospital. The report spooked him, but it also put his antennas up and kept him on his toes.

"Ooooh, this disguise is a good idea then, huh, Cousin Jabar?" He smirked.

"Yeah," he patted him on the shoulder and hung his arm around his shoulder, kissing him on the side of the head. He genuinely had love for the young nigga. He was just a manipulative piece of shit. "Here's what chu gotta remember while you're out there 'cause I'm not gonna be there witchu: you don't talk to anybody about anything. I don't give a fuck what the reasoning is, okay?" Ronie nodded his understanding. "Also, if you get snatched up by the people that are looking for me and the baby, don't tell 'em where me and the baby are. You got that?"

Ronie nodded and said, "Yeah. I got it."

"Good." He helped him slip on his jacket and handed him the car keys. "Be easy, lil' nigga, I love yo lil' punk butt."

"I love you too, cuzzo."

"And remember, you're getting pampers and Enfamil."

"I got chu."

"Babe, it's that time of the month, so I'm gonna need a few feminine products." Yada broke the news to her husband.

"Ok, well, we can hit up this CVS that's coming up right here and get chu whatever you need."

"You think you can run in and get everything for me?" she looked at him with sad puppy dog eyes. He grinned at her and nodded. They'd been out all day and night hanging up missing person photos of the baby and asking around about him. So he knew she was exhausted. This is why he agreed to go ahead and go inside of the store and purchase the items she needed.

"Thank you, baby." She kissed him.

"You're welcome, ma." He pulled into the CVS parking lot and parked his vehicle. Right then, Voss' cell phone rung and he looked at its display, seeing that it was a blocked number. He wasn't going to answer it at first, but something told him he ought to. He accepted the call and placed the cellular to his ear.

"What's up? Who dis?" Voss asked.

"This is the nigga that has your baby boy." Jabar spoke through his voice changer device. Upon hearing this, Voss frowned up and balled his hand into a fist.

"I'm listening."

"If you want junior here back, I'mma need two mill large delivered to..." he went on to give him the address of where he was to drop the bag of money to. "You get all of that, or do I need to repeat myself."

"Nah, I got it. You want two million dropped to the address you gave me at 9 o'clock tomorrow night. Show up alone, or you start mailing my kid to me in pieces."

"Good, boy," Jabar disconnected the call.

Yada sighed with relief knowing that she'd be in contact with her baby once they dropped the bag on Jabar. "All we have to do is give this nigga the bag he wants and we can get our son back."

"Once I get the few things outta here, we'll shoot to the house and get the money outta the safe. Then we'll shoot up there to make the exchange. We've gotta 'bouta," he looked at the time on his cellular. "Two hours. Two hours before we've gotta meet up with this nigga. I'll be right back out so we can shoot back to the crib. I love you." He kissed her lips.

"I love you, too, babe. Hurry back." She told him, holding his hand.

"I will, ma." He kissed her on the forehead and jumped out of the car, slamming the door shut behind him. He made his way across the parking lot and inside of CVS where the ding sounded as soon as he crossed the threshold, heading to the area where they kept the feminine products.

Tranay Adams

CHAPTER SEVEN

While Voss was busy looking for the items that Yada request-ed, a strange man approached him. He was wearing cornrows and a bushy beard that looked like it belonged on a hillbilly. The dude claimed not to know which pampers were the best so he asked him. Voss didn't know which pampers were the best either, but he figured the pampers that absorbed the most was best. So he told old boy exactly what he had in mind.

"Thank you." A disguised Ronie told Voss.

"You're welcome." A frowned-up Voss said. He noticed the scar that he had over his eyebrow and eyelids. When the man turned to walk away, he spotted the six AK-47 bullets tattooed on the side of the neck. That's when he imagined the stranger without the beard and cornrows and he looked exactly like Ronan Percy. The mothafucka that appeared on television as one of the suspects in the UCLA hospital massacre.

"It's you, you!" Voss scowled and charged Ronie.

A frightened Ronie turned around with a surprised look on his face. He went to pull his gun and start busting, but Voss was on him like flies on dookie. He fired on his mouth so hard that the ends of his cornrows jumped. As soon as he fell to the floor, Voss straddled him and started firing on his face with all of his might, dotting his clothing and face with blood. He would have killed him if it wasn't for patrons pulling him off of him.

"Lemme go, lemme the fuck go!" Voss struggled and kicked trying to get away, but his efforts were useless. All he could do was watch helplessly as Ronie scrambled to his feet and ran out of the store. Finally, Voss broke free and went after him. He cleared the threshold and darted across the parking lot to his car, popping the trunk. He snatched the M-16 out of the trunk and ran to the driver's door, snatching it open.

"Babe, what's the matter? What's going on?" Yada asked.

Voss jumped inside of the car, behind the wheel, passing the M-16 he'd gotten out of the trunk to his wife. "That mothafucka knows where our baby is!"

"What, are you sure?"

"I swear on his life."

"Well, get 'em, catch up to 'em!" Yada told Voss as he whipped out of the parking spot and jetted out of there. She checked the banana clip of the assault rifle and smacked it back into the weapon. She then shut one of her eyelids and checked the range sighting on it. Afterwards, she let her window down and repositioned herself in the seat, gripping the M-16 with both hands.

Vroooom!

Ronie ripped up the street dipping in and out of traffic, passing cars. He glanced over his shoulder continuously, trying to see where the guy he'd bumped into at the store was. He thought he'd lost him until he saw him dipping in and out of lanes, speeding up to where he was in traffic.

"Fuck, fuck, fuck, fuck!" Ronie smacked himself upside the head with his handgun, knowing he'd fucked up.

Jabar had told him before he left the house to avoid talking to anyone and he had managed to fuck that up…royally. "Cousin Jabar is gonna be mad at me! Cousin Jabar is gonna be really, really, really mad at me!" he started crying and whining, snot threatening to drip from his right nostril.

He popped open the glove box and grabbed his handgun, cocking a copper bullet into its head. When he glanced into the sideview mirror and saw Voss' speeding vehicle, he became anxious and rolled his window down. Keeping his eyes on the street, he stuck his gun out of the window and started busting. Bullets whizzed through the air. Some of them missed Voss' car while others struck its windshield and hood causing the vehicle to swerve out of control.

***

120

"Babe, are you all right? Are you okay?" Voss asked Yada. Ronie had just sent some hot shit at them which went through the windshield and narrowly missed them.

"Yes, yes," Yada nodded rapidly. "I'm fine. I'm okay. Speed up so I can blast his ass though. That punk, bitch ass mothafucka!"

"Nah, you can't kill 'em. If you kill 'em then we'll never find out where they're holding the baby."

"Okay. You're right. What do we do?"

"I'mma get as close as I can to 'em, you shoot out his tires. Once his ho ass crashes, we'll snatch 'em up, okay?" he looked at her.

"Okay." She nodded yes, getting a firmer grip of her M-16.

Voss and Yada kissed romantically. Once they got that out of the way, Voss mashed the gas pedal and the car flew down the block, leaving debris in its wake. The lines in the road turned into blurs the vehicle was moving so fast. Before Voss and Yada knew it their car was close to lining up beside Ronie's. At this time, Yada eased halfway outside of the car window, hair and clothes ruffling as the wind blew against her. She narrowed her eyelids into slits and hoisted up the M-16, taking aim at the front tire of Ronie's vehicle.

"You got it?" Voss asked as he looked back and forth between the windshield and his wife. When she didn't answer he asked her again. "Babe, I asked did you have it?"

Yada had one of her eyelids shut as she aimed for the front tire of Ronie's vehicle. A minute passed before she finally answered, saying, "Unh huh. I've got it."

Yada pulled the trigger of the rifle and a sharp jacketed bullet exploded from out of the barrel. The bullet came out of whizzing, going at a speed that seemed like slow motion, entering the front tire of Ronie's vehicle and causing it to erupt. Ronie screamed and hollered like a bitch as he struggled to regain control of his car. The vehicle flipped three times before sliding on its rooftop, bumping up against a telephone pole, stopping.

Urrrrrrk!

Voss mashed the brake pedal and brought his whip to an abrupt halt. He hopped out of his car click clacking one into the head of his handgun. Yada jumped out of the car right behind him, still gripping her M-16 with both hands. She moved in on the flipped vehicle that Ronie was inside of like she was military trained. Voss came up from behind her gripping his handgun with both hands, moving with the skill of his wife.

"I'll watch cho back, boo, you watch my front." Yada told her man. He swept in front of her with his handgun, watching the front of Ronie's car carefully. He was startled when Ronie stuck his bloody hands out of the busted-out windshield, waving them around and asking for help.

"I surrender! Help! Somebody help me, please!" Ronie called out.

Seeing that Ronie was harmless, Voss tucked his gun at the small of his back. He then walked upon the windshield and drug Ronie out by his collar, sliding his ass across the broken glass scattered on the street.

"Oh, thank you, thank you, thank you!" Ronie said over and over again as Voss pulled him back upon his feet. He then shoved him up against his car. Holding him at the collar of his shirt, he punched him in the gut three times and punched him across the jaw. Blood sprayed through the air and Ronie dropped on his ass. Voss grabbed the rooftop of the car and started stomping homeboy in his face and chest, getting blood on his sneaker and shit.

"Punk ass mothafucka, gon' take my son! My fucking prince! You got me fucked up, homeboy." Voss yanked Ronie to his feet, kneeing him in his balls and then head-butting his nose.

The impact from his forehead busted his nose and bloodied his mouth, causing blood to drip from it. Voss turned Ronie around roughly and told him to place his hands on the rooftop of the car which he did. Voss then turned to Yada and told her to keep her M-16 on his ass. She obliged him.

Voss popped the trunk and grabbed the duct tape. Coming back around the car, he duct-taped Ronie's wrists behind his back and smacked a strip of duct tape over his mouth. Afterwards, Voss grabbed him roughly by the back of his neck and hustled him over to the rear of the car, tossing him into the back of the trunk. Once he'd deposited homeboy in the trunk, Voss slammed the trunk shut and walked over to his wife, smacking imaginary dirt from his hands. "Come on, lil' mama, we're taking this piece of shit to The House of Pain, and he's gonna tell us where our baby boy is."

Yada jumped into the front passenger seat of her man's car and slammed the door shut. Voss sped off down the street, dialing up Marla. He had her meet him at The House of Pain. She didn't know what that place was, so he explained it to her and gave her the address to the place. Voss parked into the backyard and got Ronie out of the trunk, hustling through the back door of the house. He and Yada then helped him down the staircase into the basement where they shackled his wrists, with his back to them. Voss tore open the back of Ronie's shirt and exposed his bony back. He then grabbed a nearby whip that was hanging from a large nail in the wall. He thrashed the whip open and beat Ronie's back until it was bloody and swollen. Each time he gave him a lashing he told him to tell him where Jabar was at with his baby, but the young man refused to tell him.

"This son of a bitch is as tough as a bucket of old rusty nails." Voss told Yada as he turned to her. His face and upper body was covered in beads of sweat. He was exhausted from whipping Ronie's back.

"I don't think it's just that. He's mentally handicap. He doesn't comprehend everything that's going on here." Yada added her two cents. "It's like he has the mind of a child."

"Hmmmm," Voss massaged his chin as he thought on something. "If what you're saying is true, then I'm sure homeboy told him something so that he'd never tell us where the baby is. So since we can't get 'em to tell us where the baby is, maybe we can get 'em to lure Jabar and the baby to us."

"What chu got cooking under that lid?" Gerardo asked, referring to what he was thinking. He'd gotten out of jail on bail the day prior, but he still hadn't gone to go to trial.

"Oh, I got a lil' something, something." Voss cracked a grin. He then looked up at Ronie. "Say, bruh, what do you like to eat, candy?"

"Ca, candy? I, I love candy. I love Starburst, cherry Starburst." Ronie continued to cry, tears dripping to the floor. His left eye was swollen shut and his face was swollen and bloody. That nigga Voss had really put that ass in the hurt locker.

"Okay, check this out, Ronie, since you can't take me to where Jabar and the baby are, you can call 'em and have 'em come to you. You do that and I'll give you three cherry Starburst." He held up three fingers. "How would you like that?" he cracked him a smile, looking crazy as fuck with all of his blood splattered on him.

"Yes, yes, I can do that." Ronie nodded.

"Okay. I'll get chu down, clean you up and you call 'em." Voss told him. He then released him from the shackles and took him into the bathroom where he had Yada and Marla wash him up and rinse him off. While they were doing this, he threw his clothing in the washer and then the dryer. Once the clothing had dried, he tossed them to Ronie and he put them on. Afterwards, Voss told Ronie what to say once Jabar picked up the jack. He then took out Ronie's cellular and hit up Jabar, passing the cell phone back to him.

As soon as Jabar picked up the jack, Ronie gave him some bullshit story about how a cop pulled him over and recognized him so he had to kill him. He then told him he needed his help burying the pig inside of the woods. Jabar went for the story.

He asked for directions how to get there and Voss whispered in Ronie's ear what to say. Once the conversation ended, Voss took the cell phone and disconnected the call.

***

Ronie stood out in the middle of the woods. Voss put his hood over his head and pulled the drawstrings of his hoodie, enclosing it around his head, to cover up as much of Ronie's face as he could. Voss knew that if Jabar saw how fucked up Ronie's face was that he'd know that something was up and then their plan would be shot to shit. Voss wanted Jabar's ass like a young nigga wanted pussy on prom night. So he wasn't trying to fuck this up.

Jabar pulled his whip before his cousin. He murdered the engine but left the headlights on so that they could see in the dark when they went to bury the cop he'd killed. Jabar hopped out of the car smoking the roach end of a blunt. He blew out a cloud of smoke and dropped what was left of his Backwood at his foot, mashing the shit out. As he approached Ronie, all the nigga could make out was his silhouette as he advanced in his direction. It wasn't until he was right up on him that he could partially see his face.

"Yo, let's hurry up and bury this mothafucka so we can get up outta here," Jabar said as he pulled on a pair of thick, gray working gloves. His face frowned up and he looked closely at Ronie's face. Grasping his chin, he turned his face from left to right, taking in the stock from the damage that was done. Jabar then took in his cousin's body as a whole and noticed the nigga was trembling. "What the fuck is up witchu, man?" Ronie didn't say shit. He shook harder so he turned his face so that he could face him. That's when he saw the tears dripping from the brims of his eyes.

"I'm sorry, cuzzo." Ronie apologized and dropped his head, teardrops falling from his eyes and splashing on the brittle leaves below him.

As soon as Ronie said he was sorry, Jabar's eyes grew big and his mouth dropped open. He looked to the ground and the illumination coming from the headlights shone on the trees and cast the shadows of niggaz holding AK-47s in hiding. Right then, Jabar went to pull his banga from the small of his back as he backed up to take cover behind his car. It was too late for him though because Voss, Gerardo, Marla and Yada was on him like flies on shit. They came out from where they were hiding behind the trees and ran up on Jabar just as he was pointing his gun to open fire. Before he could curl his finger around his .9mm handgun, everyone was already opening up on him.

Blatatatatatat, blatatatatat, blatatatatatat, blatatatatatatat, blatatatatatatat!

Jabar dropped his handgun and danced on his feet as bullets flew in and out of him, splattering his blood on the leaves and trees surrounding him. When the AK-47s stopped firing, Jabar was still on his feet, smoking from all of the hot lead he was pumped with. Suddenly, he fell flat on his back, lying still but moving his head from left to right to see who his killaz were. Voss was the first to approach him followed by the others, kicking his .9mm handgun out of reach of him. Once Voss and the others were standing over Jabar they could see his eyes twinkling with tears in them and the pain in his face as he winced, his hands animatedly grasping the brittle leaves on the ground and crushing them.

"Kill me, kill me, kill me, fuck nigga! Get the shit over with!" Jabar told a mad dogging Voss, keeping his gangsta intact, spitting up blood. He'd be damned if he went out like a ho.

Voss lowered his AK-47 and pulled a gun from the small of his back, calling Ronie over. When Ronie approached him, he gave him his gun and everyone looked at him like he was nuts. But he didn't give a fuck though. This was how he wanted this shit to go down.

"Finish yo punk ass cousin, Blood!" Voss told him.

Ronie wiped the dripping tears from his eyes with the back of his hand and pointed his gun down at his cousin's forehead. He couldn't stop the tears from flowing down his face as he held the gun on his loved one who was like a brother to him. He didn't know how he'd be able to live with himself if he pulled the trigger, but he did know if he did pull it, he'd still be alive, not dead.

"This how you do me, nigga? Huh, yo own, yo own flesh and blood? Let niggaz turn you against me? Fuck you, fuck you, you ain't my family!" Jabar spit blood at Ronie and it splattered on the leg of his jeans. By this time, Ronie was sobbing and sounding like a straight up ho.

"Fuck this nigga, man! Pop 'em!" Voss said to Ronie.

"Yeah, pop 'em 'fore we pop yo ass!" Yada told him.

"Gone and smoke 'em!" Gerardo jabbed Ronie in his back with his AK-47 causing his body to jerk.

"Hurry up!" Marla also jabbed him with her AK-47.

A moment later, Ronie turned the gun that Voss had given him on Voss and pulled the trigger. The gun clicked empty and a surprised look came over Ronie's face. He looked at the gun and then back at Voss who was smiling wickedly. Voss popped him in his chest with the AK-47 and he dropped into the leaves on the ground, causing them to crunch beneath them. Everyone else stood over him and sprayed his ass.

Blatatatatat, blatatatatat, blatatatatatat, blatatatatatatat, blatatatatatatat!

Ronie's body looked like it was break dancing on its back as it was sprayed with deadly ammunition. Once the gunfire stopped, Ronie lie still wearing the Face of Death, body smoking from the hot bullets that were sprayed at him. Voss and everyone else then turned their AK-47s on Jabar and sprayed his ass again, making sure he was dead this time.

A look came over Yada's face like she'd just remembered something and she dropped her AK-47, running towards Jabar's vehicle. She pulled open the driver's door and looked upfront, she opened the back-passenger door and the baby wasn't in there.

Yada pulled her head out of the car and looked up at everyone else who was running towards her, saying, "He's not here! He's not here!" she wept and wept jumping up and down.

Her family came running towards her as she dipped inside of the front seat and popped the trunk, running to the rear of the vehicle. She lifted the trunk and started taking out all of the stuff that she saw inside. Still, there wasn't any baby inside of the trunk. Right then, defeated, Yada dropped down to her knees and covered her face with both of her hands. Her vision became obscured as fresh tears built up in her eyes. Tears poured down her face as her entire body shook. She cried and cried.

Voss passed his AK-47 to Gerardo and dropped down to his knees beside Yada. He hugged her close and rubbed her back, comforting her. Tears formed in Voss' eyes thinking he'd never find his child, but he couldn't let Yada see him in distress.

"Shhhhhhhh," Voss tried his best to comfort his wife, kissing her on top of the head. "Everything is going to be all right, okay? We're gonna find our lil' man. I swear to you. We're gonna find 'em."

"Oh, my God, my baby boy, my sweet, sweet, baby boy." Yada cried aloud, face soaked and bottom lip trembling. "God, why my child? Why my son? Why, Lord, why? Tell me why?"

Gerardo and Marla hugged one another as they stared at their son and daughter, Voss and Yada. Marla cried silently and Gerardo comforted her as best as he could, trying his best to sooth her grieving. It broke their hearts seeing Voss and Yada in so much emotional strain.

Dawn

Voss, Yada, Marla and Gerardo stood inside of the junk yard. They were looking up at Nonsense who was sitting inside of the machine that operated the magnetic crane. You see, Nonsense was Gerardo's homeboy who actually owned and worked at the junk yard. And he was nice enough to crush Jabar's vehicle to get rid of any evidence of Jabar's whereabouts. They'd already buried Jabar and Ronie in the woods, so getting rid of the car was the last thing on their agenda.

With the sway of his hand, Nonsense motioned for Voss, Yada, Marla and Gerardo to clear the path for him to grab hold of the Jabar's vehicle. Once they were out of the way, Nonsense brought the magnet over the rooftop of the car. The whip shook a little, which disturbed the pebbles on the ground it was parked on. Suddenly, the automobile slammed upward into the magnet.

Nonsense switched up the levers inside of the machine and brought the automobile over to the car crusher. As the whip was craned over to the car crusher, everyone could hear the faint cries of a baby. Voss, Yada, Marla and Gerardo exchanged glances.

"Did y'all hear that?" Voss asked everyone.

"Yeah." Everyone nodded and said.

"Waa, waa, waa, waa, waa!"

"There it is again, y'all!" Voss announced.

"It's the baby!" Yada ran over to where Nonsense could see her, waving her arms and jumping up and down, trying to make sure that she could be seen.

"My baby, my baby is somewhere inside of the car! You've gotta put the car down!" she called out through her cupped hands, sounding like she was speaking through a megaphone.

"Waa, waa, waa, waa, waa!"

Yada looked up into the sky as tears spilled out of her eyes, with her hands interlocked, pleading, "Please, God, I'm begging you, let my child be alright. Let 'em be okay."

Nonsense nodded his head. He swung the car back around and sat it on the ground. At this time, Yada and everyone else was running over to the vehicle. Voss reached inside of the whip and popped the trunk open. He then ran to the rear of the car, opening up the trunk. There wasn't anything inside like there wasn't before and the baby's crying had grown silent. A minute later the baby started back crying again. That's when it dawned on Voss that he didn't check the spare tire compartment. He opened up the compartment and found the baby. Jabar must have put him there in case he got pulled over and couldn't explain the child to the police.

"I've got 'em, I've got V.J.!" Voss announced.

Gerardo and Marla hugged and kissed each other jumping up and down, happy that their grandson had been found.

Voss picked up the baby and passed him to his smiling and crying mother. Yada rubbed her nose against her child and kissed him all over his face. She then hugged him against her and pulled Voss into her. They all hugged up, crying and smiling.

"I overheard you call the baby V.J. Does that stand for Voss junior? Is that what you'd like to name 'em?" Yada asked Voss.

"Yeah, V.J," Voss smiled, thinking about the encounter he had with an older version of his son in his dream.

Gerardo and Marla walked over to Voss, Yada and the baby, wrapping their arms around them and staring down at little V.J. excitedly.

THE END

Submission Guideline

Submit the first three chapters of your completed manuscript to ldpsubmissions@gmail.com, subject line: Your book's title. The manuscript must be in a .doc file and sent as an attachment. Document should be in Times New Roman, double spaced and in size 12 font. Also, provide your synopsis and full contact information. If sending multiple submissions, they must each be in a separate email.

Have a story but no way to send it electronically? You can still submit to LDP/Ca$h Presents. Send in the first three chapters, written or typed, of your completed manuscript to:

LDP: Submissions Dept
Po Box 870494
Mesquite, Tx 75187

DO NOT send original manuscript. Must be a duplicate.

Provide your synopsis and a cover letter containing your full contact information.

Thanks for considering LDP and Ca$h Presents.

Tranay Adams

Coming Soon from Lock Down Publications/Ca$h Presents

BOW DOWN TO MY GANGSTA
By **Ca$h**
TORN BETWEEN TWO
By **Coffee**
BLOOD STAINS OF A SHOTTA **III**
By **Jamaica**
STEADY MOBBIN **III**
By **Marcellus Allen**
BLOOD OF A BOSS **VI**
By **Askari**
LOYAL TO THE GAME **IV**
LIFE OF SIN **III**
By **T.J. & Jelissa**
A DOPEBOY'S PRAYER **II**
By **Eddie "Wolf" Lee**
IF LOVING YOU IS WRONG… **III**
LOVE ME EVEN WHEN IT HURTS **III**
By **Jelissa**
TRUE SAVAGE **VII**
By **Chris Green**
BLAST FOR ME **III**
DUFFLE BAG CARTEL **IV**
By **Ghost**
ADDICTIED TO THE DRAMA **III**
By **Jamila Mathis**

132

A HUSTLER'S DECEIT 3

KILL ZONE **II**

BAE BELONGS TO ME III

SOUL OF A MONSTER

By **Aryanna**

THE COST OF LOYALTY **III**

By **Kweli**

SHE FELL IN LOVE WITH A REAL ONE **II**

By **Tamara Butler**

RENEGADE BOYS **III**

By **Meesha**

CORRUPTED BY A GANGSTA **IV**

By **Destiny Skai**

A GANGSTER'S SYN II

By **J-Blunt**

KING OF NEW YORK V

RISE TO POWER III

COKE KINGS II

By **T.J. Edwards**

GORILLAZ IN THE BAY III

De'Kari

THE STREETS ARE CALLING II

Duquie Wilson

KINGPIN KILLAZ IV

STREET KINGS 2

PAID IN BLOOD 2

Hood Rich

SINS OF A HUSTLA II

ASAD

TRIGGADALE II

Elijah R. Freeman

MARRIED TO A BOSS III

By Destiny Skai & Chris Green

KINGS OF THE GAME III

Playa Ray

SLAUGHTER GANG II

By Willie Slaughter

<u>Available Now</u>

<u>RESTRAINING ORDER **I & II**</u>

By **CA$H & Coffee**

<u>LOVE KNOWS NO BOUNDARIES **I II & III**</u>

By **Coffee**

<u>RAISED AS A GOON I, II, III & IV</u>

<u>BRED BY THE SLUMS I, II, III</u>

<u>BLAST FOR ME I & II</u>

<u>ROTTEN TO THE CORE I III</u>

<u>A BRONX TALE I, II, III</u>

<u>DUFFEL BAG CARTEL I II III</u>

By **Ghost**

<u>LAY IT DOWN **I & II**</u>

<u>LAST OF A DYING BREED</u>

<u>BLOOD STAINS OF A SHOTTA I & II</u>

By **Jamaica**

LOYAL TO THE GAME

LOYAL TO THE GAME II

LOYAL TO THE GAME III

LIFE OF SIN I, II

By **TJ & Jelissa**

BLOODY COMMAS I & II

SKI MASK CARTEL I II & III

KING OF NEW YORK I II,III IV

RISE TO POWER I II

COKE KINGS

By **T.J. Edwards**

IF LOVING HIM IS WRONG…I & II

LOVE ME EVEN WHEN IT HURTS I II

By **Jelissa**

WHEN THE STREETS CLAP BACK I & II III

By **Jibril Williams**

A DISTINGUISHED THUG STOLE MY HEART I II & III

LOVE SHOULDN'T HURT I II III IV

RENEGADE BOYS I & II

By **Meesha**

A GANGSTER'S CODE I &, II III

A GANGSTER'S SYN

By J-Blunt

PUSH IT TO THE LIMIT

By **Bre' Hayes**

BLOOD OF A BOSS **I, II, III, IV, V**

By **Askari**

THE STREETS BLEED MURDER **I, II & III**

THE HEART OF A GANGSTA I II& III

By **Jerry Jackson**

CUM FOR ME

CUM FOR ME 2

CUM FOR ME 3

CUM FOR ME 4

An **LDP Erotica Collaboration**

BRIDE OF A HUSTLA **I II & II**

THE FETTI GIRLS **I, II& III**

CORRUPTED BY A GANGSTA I, II & III

By **Destiny Skai**

WHEN A GOOD GIRL GOES BAD

By **Adrienne**

THE COST OF LOYALTY

By Kweli

A GANGSTER'S REVENGE **I II III & IV**

THE BOSS MAN'S DAUGHTERS

THE BOSS MAN'S DAUGHTERS II

THE BOSSMAN'S DAUGHTERS III

THE BOSSMAN'S DAUGHTERS IV

THE BOSS MAN'S DAUGHTERS **V**

A SAVAGE LOVE **I & II**

BAE BELONGS TO ME I II

A HUSTLER'S DECEIT I, II, III

WHAT BAD BITCHES DO I, II, III

By **Aryanna**

A KINGPIN'S AMBITON

A KINGPIN'S AMBITION **II**

I MURDER FOR THE DOUGH

By **Ambitious**

TRUE SAVAGE

TRUE SAVAGE II

TRUE SAVAGE **III**

TRUE SAVAGE **IV**

TRUE SAVAGE **V**

TRUE SAVAGE **VI**

By **Chris Green**

A DOPEBOY'S PRAYER

By **Eddie "Wolf" Lee**

THE KING CARTEL **I, II & III**

By **Frank Gresham**

THESE NIGGAS AIN'T LOYAL **I, II & III**

By **Nikki Tee**

GANGSTA SHYT **I II &III**

By **CATO**

THE ULTIMATE BETRAYAL

By **Phoenix**

BOSS'N UP **I , II & III**

By **Royal Nicole**

I LOVE YOU TO DEATH

By Destiny J

I RIDE FOR MY HITTA

I STILL RIDE FOR MY HITTA

By **Misty Holt**

LOVE & CHASIN' PAPER

By **Qay Crockett**

TO DIE IN VAIN

SINS OF A HUSTLA

By **ASAD**

BROOKLYN HUSTLAZ

By **Boogsy Morina**

BROOKLYN ON LOCK I & II

By **Sonovia**

GANGSTA CITY

By **Teddy Duke**

A DRUG KING AND HIS DIAMOND I & II III

A DOPEMAN'S RICHES

HER MAN, MINE'S TOO I, II

CASH MONEY HO'S

By Nicole Goosby

TRAPHOUSE KING **I II & III**

KINGPIN KILLAZ I II III

STREET KINGS

PAID IN BLOOD

By **Hood Rich**

LIPSTICK KILLAH **I, II, III**

CRIME OF PASSION I & II

By **Mimi**

STEADY MOBBN' **I, II, III**

By **Marcellus Allen**

WHO SHOT YA **I, II, III**

Renta

GORILLAZ IN THE BAY **I II**

DE'KARI

TRIGGADALE

Elijah R. Freeman

GOD BLESS THE TRAPPERS I, II, III

THESE SCANDALOUS STREETS I, II, III

FEAR MY GANGSTA I, II, III

THESE STREETS DON'T LOVE NOBODY I, II

BURY ME A G I, II, III, IV, V

A GANGSTA'S EMPIRE I, II, III, IV

Tranay Adams

THE STREETS ARE CALLING

Duquie Wilson

MARRIED TO A BOSS... I II

By Destiny Skai & Chris Green

KINGS OF THE GAME I II

Playa Ray

SLAUGHTER GANG II

By Willie Slaughter

BOOKS BY LDP'S CEO, CA$H

TRUST IN NO MAN

TRUST IN NO MAN 2

TRUST IN NO MAN 3

BONDED BY BLOOD

SHORTY GOT A THUG

THUGS CRY

THUGS CRY 2

THUGS CRY 3

TRUST NO BITCH

TRUST NO BITCH 2

TRUST NO BITCH 3

TIL MY CASKET DROPS

RESTRAINING ORDER

RESTRAINING ORDER 2

IN LOVE WITH A CONVICT

Coming Soon

BONDED BY BLOOD 2

BOW DOWN TO MY GANGSTA

www.ingramcontent.com/pod-product-compliance
Lightning Source LLC
Chambersburg PA
CBHW060426260626
47161CB00005B/1804